Mike O'Rourke was five years her junior.

He deserved a girl his own age, a younger woman who shared his white-picket-fence dreams.

Now here Simone was, facing the reality of her champagne-induced mistake.

Simone took a good, hard look at the testing apparatus that held the answer to the question that had been haunting her since the morning she'd awakened in Mike's arms.

As a mental clock tick-tocked in her brain, she watched the little pink dot grow darker by the moment.

She *was* pregnant.

With Mike O'Rourke's baby.

Available in April 2009
from Mills & Boon®
Special Edition

Once Upon a Pregnancy

JUDY DUARTE

MILLS & BOON

Pure reading pleasure™

*First published in Great Britain 2009
by Harlequin Mills & Boon Limited,
Eton House, 18-24 Paradise Road, Richmond, Surrey TW9 1SR*

© Harlequin Books S.A. 2008

*Special thanks and acknowledgement are given to Judy Duarte
for her contribution to The Wilder Family mini-series.*

ISBN: 978 0 263 87034 3

23-0409

*Harlequin Mills & Boon policy is to use papers that are
natural, renewable and recyclable products and made from
wood grown in sustainable forests. The logging and
manufacturing processes conform to the legal environmental
regulations of the country of origin.*

*Printed and bound in Spain
by Litografia Rosés S.A., Barcelona*

JUDY DUARTE

always knew there was a book inside her, but since English was her least favourite subject in school, she never considered herself a writer. An avid reader who enjoys a happy ending, Judy couldn't shake the dream of creating a book of her own.

Her dream became a reality in March of 2002, when Special Edition released her first book. Since then, she has sold nineteen more novels.

Her stories have touched the hearts of readers around the world. And in July of 2005 Judy won a prestigious Readers' Choice Award for *The Rich Man's Son*.

Judy makes her home near the beach in Southern California. When she's not cooped up in her writing cave, she's spending time with her somewhat enormous, but delightfully close, family.

To the authors who worked with me on this series – Marie Ferrarella, Mary J Forbes, Teresa Southwick, Karen Rose Smith and RaeAnne Thayne.

Thank you for making this book fun to write.

Chapter One

Simone Garner studied the home pregnancy test kit sitting on the white tile countertop in her bathroom and waited as one long second stretched into another.

She was thirty-seven years old and a nurse at Walnut River General Hospital, so she certainly should have known better than to let something like this happen.

*But…*she *had* let it happen, and there was no one to blame but herself.

Two months ago, at a cocktail party Dr. Peter Wilder hosted to celebrate the rechristening of the hospital library in honor of his late father, a waiter holding a tray of champagne approached Simone and offered her a glass.

A teetotaler by nature, she nearly declined, but the festive mood had been contagious.

At first, the champagne hadn't done much for her

except to tickle her nose and throat, but she'd soon acquired a taste for it, as well as a mind-numbing buzz.

So when Mike O'Rourke, an attractive medic she'd known for a while, volunteered to drive her home, she'd agreed. Then, while he opened the door to let her into his Jeep, she'd let him kiss her.

Or maybe she'd been the instigator.

Looking back, she wasn't entirely sure who'd actually made the first move. All she knew was that the star-spinning, knee-weakening kiss had happened.

After they arrived at her place, she should have thanked him for the ride and let it go at that, but for some reason, she felt compelled to invite him in. She'd given him a tour of the house she'd remodeled, then turned on her new stereo system and played a soft, suggestive love song.

"Do you want to dance?"

Her boldness had been so out of character that, in retrospect, she'd blamed her newfound self-confidence on the alcohol, as well as the sleek black cocktail dress she'd purchased for the occasion and the cute but impractical heels she'd probably only wear once.

With her senses still reeling from both the champagne and Mike's charm, Simone had slipped into his embrace, quickly relishing his musky, mountain-fresh scent and the faint bristle of his cheek against hers.

They'd swayed to the soul-stirring melody, hearts beating and bodies moving as one—until she'd stumbled.

She'd grabbed on to Mike for balance, and they'd shared a laugh, followed by a heated look, a lingering touch.

One thing had led to another, and they'd kissed again.

Oh, Lordy, how they'd kissed.

Then, for some crazy reason—the heat of the moment, she supposed—she'd led him to her bedroom.

Waking up in Mike's arms and then sending him on his way would have been a lot easier to do if their love-making had only been so-so. In that case, he would have understood why she'd ended things.

But the entire experience had been off the charts.

And now she feared that if great sex had anything to do with sperm motility or fertility, she'd be having septuplets.

Oh, God, no. *Please,* no.

Just the thought of what a pink dot on the testing apparatus meant made her nauseous, even though she'd already had the dry heaves earlier this morning.

At first, she'd told herself that stress from work had caused her period to be delayed. After all, there had been some allegations of insurance fraud at Walnut River General, and the timing couldn't be worse, with the hospital in danger of being taken over by Northeastern HealthCare.

And to top it off, someone was leaking financial information and other sensitive data to the conglomerate, putting the hospital at a significant disadvantage for negotiations.

But Simone hadn't been able to explain away her symptoms any longer. So she got up from her seat on the commode and stood before the test, while her future and the pale yellow walls of the small bathroom seemed to close in on her.

No pink dot yet, though.

Maybe it *had* been stress. Maybe her conscience and

her imagination had become a tag team and were really doing a number on her, punishing her for allowing herself one little sexual fantasy.

After all, she and Mike had used condoms, but, looking back, she had to admit they'd gotten a little careless with their use as the night wore on.

She blew out a sigh, then glanced at her wristwatch, realizing it was silly to second-guess the test results when she'd know for sure in a few more minutes.

Nevertheless, she wasn't the kind of woman she'd pretended to be and couldn't help feeling foolish for her lack of self-control.

Over the past five weeks, she'd rationalized about what she'd done at least a hundred times, telling herself she was a healthy woman with sexual needs that hadn't been satisfied in a long time. And that she couldn't help having a one-night stand with the dark-haired paramedic who was too sexy for his own good—or rather, for *her* own good.

But Mike O'Rourke was five years her junior. And he deserved a girl his own age, a younger woman who shared his white-picket-fence dreams.

Now, here Simone was, facing the reality of her champagne-induced mistake.

If her suspicion was right, if she was pregnant, she would make an appointment with Mark Kipper, one of the doctors in the Walnut River OB/GYN Medical Group. She was determined to do whatever it took to make sure the child was as healthy as possible.

A thump sounded against the door, followed by a bark and a whine.

"Hold on, Woofer," she told the big, clumsy mutt

who demanded her time when she was home. "I'll be out in a minute."

Each day after a trying but satisfying shift at the hospital, she went home and was met at the gate by the ugly but lovable dog she'd adopted through an animal-rescue group.

Finding Woofer and bringing him home had been a fluke that had proven to be a blessing for both woman and dog, even if there were times she missed her privacy and freedom.

But at least she could put Woofer out in the backyard to entertain himself with butterflies and chew toys while she was at work. She certainly couldn't do that with a baby.

Simone took a good hard look at the testing apparatus that held the answer to the question that had been haunting her since the morning she'd awakened in Mike's arms.

As a mental clock ticktocked in her brain, she watched the little pink dot grow darker by the moment. Then she blew out a ragged sigh of resignation.

She *was* pregnant.

With Mike O'Rourke's baby.

What the hell was she going to do?

There was no telling how the handsome paramedic was going to feel about this. She suspected the news might blow that crush to kingdom come—a good thing, actually. But still, Simone was in no hurry to tell him.

"Ar-oof." Woofer's tail thump, thump, thumped against the door. "Ar-oof, ar-oof."

That darn dog could be such a baby sometimes.

In fact, he was the only baby a woman like Simone ought to have. Which was why there was only one option for her to consider…adoption.

As she watched the dot turn a deeper shade of pink, her uneasiness grew by leaps and bounds.

Mike wanted more out of their professional relationship than friendship, and ever since they'd made love, he'd been even more determined than ever to be a part of her life.

If he weren't such a nice guy, if he didn't make her laugh like no one else could, she would have given him the cold shoulder and completely shut him out until he saw reason and left her alone.

It was a ploy she had perfected in the past, an easy ruse that had come with the old baggage she carried from childhood.

But she'd never been able to fully shoot an icy glare at Mike. He'd just been too sweet, too charming.

Another thump sounded on the bathroom door, followed by a loud bark. "Okay, Woofer. We'll take a walk. Just give me a—"

The doorbell rang, and Woofer took off, howling up a storm, his paws clomping across the hardwood floor of the small, cozy house.

"Oh, great," she muttered, assuming a neighbor or possibly a salesman was at the door. "I'm coming!"

She left the pregnancy test in the bathroom, its pink dot shining like a beacon, and headed for the entry, where she would have to run interference between the person knocking and her four-legged roommate.

Woofer might look and sound like one heck of a guard dog, when in truth, he was a real softie. If confronted with a burglar, he'd probably knock him to the floor and lick him to death.

When she reached the door and peered through the

peephole at the man on the front porch, instant recognition caused her heart to drop to the pit of her stomach.

There stood Mike O'Rourke, as big and gorgeous as you please. He wore a pair of faded Levi's, a navy-blue T-shirt that displayed a white Walnut River Fire Department logo across his chest and a heart-stopping grin.

In his hands, he held a cardboard box.

What was *he* doing here?

"Just a minute." She grabbed Woofer's collar and pulled him back so she could get a hold of the knob. Hopefully, the screen door would prevent the dog from dive-bombing Mike and knocking him on his butt, which more than one E.R. nurse had admired behind his back—a butt that Simone had learned was even more noteworthy bare.

She swung open the wooden door, leaving the screen to separate them.

Mike, with his black hair stylishly mussed and his green eyes sparkling, shifted the box he held from one side to the other. "I brought you something. Can you put Woofer in the backyard for a couple of minutes?"

He'd brought her something?

Well, it certainly wasn't flowers. Or chocolate, which seemed like the kind of romantic gift he might offer her.

"Give me a minute, will you?" She grabbed Woofer by the collar again. "I'll be right back." Then she led the dog to the kitchen and opened the back door, encouraging him to romp in the yard.

But Woofer wasn't happy about missing the excitement of having a guest, and Simone, on the other hand, wasn't all that thrilled about having Mike O'Rourke stop by, especially today.

Of course, she supposed it wouldn't hurt to sit outside with Mike on the front porch for a little while and chat.

But when she heard the hinges of the screen door creak open, followed by footsteps on the hardwood floor, her senses reeled and her tummy took a tumble.

She didn't need to consult a psychologist or social worker to figure out why.

Not with that home pregnancy test propped up on her bathroom counter, the results as obvious as a pink neon sign.

Mike couldn't imagine that Simone had expected him to stand on the stoop like a pizza deliveryman. And although she hadn't exactly invited him into the house, she was putting Woofer in the backyard, and she'd said she would be right back.

So he'd entered the living room, took a seat on the pale green sofa and waited for her to return.

Actually, what he'd brought her wasn't exactly a gift—unless she wanted to keep it, which, he guessed, would be okay.

He glanced down at the cardboard box with the airholes he'd poked in the lid. He was in a bind, and the first person he'd thought about was Simone, who had a soft spot for animals.

After all, she'd not only opened her heart and home to Woofer, a brown, mop-haired dog who stood a slam-dunk chance to win an ugly-pet contest, but she also treated him as though he had a pedigree and was destined for nobility.

The night Mike had driven Simone home from the cocktail party, she'd invited him in and introduced him to the oversize, gangly mutt that couldn't walk across the floor without his hind end doing a hokeypokey shake to the right.

"That's got to be the ugliest dog I've ever seen," Mike had said.

"I know," she'd responded with a pride-tinged voice. "That's exactly why I adopted him. He needed a home more than any of the other dogs. Besides, he's a real sweetheart."

At that point, Simone had turned to Woofer and given him a big hug, which had caused the hem of her dress to hike up and reveal a lovely expanse of her upper thigh.

A smile had stretched across Mike's face, but not just because of the sexy flash of skin. It was the glimpse he'd gotten of the *real* Simone Garner that evening that had turned his heart on end. A fun-loving, brown-haired beauty that the no-nonsense nurse kept locked away.

Most of the medical staff at Walnut River General, as well as a lot of the guys at the department, thought Simone was cold and distant, but Mike knew the dedicated E.R. nurse better than anyone and saw things in her no one else did.

Sure, she could be aloof at times, but Mike suspected she'd been hurt by someone in the past—and badly. He also believed that if anyone could help her heal and forget about the pain, it was him.

When he first met her a few years ago, it was on a professional level. He and his partner had brought in a teenage girl who'd been the victim of a hit-and-run. The seriously injured teen had been in severe pain and was screaming for her mom, who'd yet to be identified or notified.

Simone had begun talking softly to her at first,

soothing the teen's fears, while doing her job and getting a name and number for the mother.

Mike had walked away from the E.R. that night with a great deal of respect for her. Respect had given way to admiration, and over the course of the year, Mike had taken a long, hard fall for her.

There'd even been a time or two when he'd caught her looking at him, passion clearly brewing in those soulful brown eyes. A guy didn't misread something like that.

Yet even though he knew she felt something for him too, she'd turned down each of his attempts to date her.

Then came the cocktail party that Dr. Peter Wilder had hosted.

Simone had been a warm and sexy woman that night, her walls and her legion of defense mechanisms down for the count.

But she'd soon grown distant, claiming it had all been a mistake and referring to what they'd experienced as a one-night stand.

As soft footsteps sounded, he glanced up and smiled.

But she didn't return the friendly greeting. Instead, she seemed nervous, agitated and slightly unbalanced.

Of course, she'd been acting that way around him ever since they'd slept together. So maybe he shouldn't read too much into it.

She nodded at the box he held. "What do you have in there?"

He untucked the lid and pulled out a sleepy puppy, its black-and-white coat soft and curly. It didn't take a blood test to determine that it had various quantities of cocker spaniel, poodle and terrier DNA.

"Oh my gosh. He's darling." Simone started toward

Mike, then stiffened and froze. "Wait a minute. You said you brought me something. I hope you're not thinking that I'd consider taking in another dog."

"Well, I didn't exactly plan to give little Wags to you permanently, but he and I really do need your help."

She tilted her head slightly to the side. "What's going on?"

He held the puppy close, and it nuzzled against him, then gave him a lick. "I was out jogging yesterday and found this poor little guy wandering on the dirt trail near the river. He's too young to be alone like that. And since we weren't near any neighborhoods, it was obvious that he'd been abandoned. So I couldn't just leave him there."

Her stance softened—just a bit.

"I ended my run right there, then took him home. I even checked with the animal shelter, but so far, no one has reported him missing."

She looked at the puppy, which was squirming to get down and start checking out its new surroundings.

"Poor little guy." Simone reached out and scratched its head. "I wonder who would abandon him like that."

"That's why I decided to keep him," Mike admitted.

She looked up and caught his gaze. "Then why is he *here?*"

"Because right now, I'm sharing a house with Leif, and when I took Wags home, I found out that Leif is allergic to pet dander. So if I'm going to keep him, I'll have to find another place to live sooner than I anticipated. I'll also need someone to keep him for me until then."

"And that someone is *me?*" She stroked one of the puppy's ears.

Good, she was beginning to warm and, hopefully, to bond. "Leif's sister is a real estate agent, and she's going to search the MLS listing for something in my price range."

Of course, even if the agent found something that Mike liked, escrows took time. So he was hoping Simone wouldn't mind puppy-sitting for quite a while.

"Here." Mike handed Wags to Simone. "What do you think? My options are limited, and I can't just dump him at a pet-boarding place when he's so young."

Okay, so that wasn't entirely true. Mike did have other options. He could find the puppy another home, maybe with one of the firefighters at the department. Surely someone would want him. After all, a puppy as cute as Wags stood a heck of a lot better chance at being adopted than Woofer. But there was no need to mention that to Simone. Not when Mike was hoping she'd take the fluffy, black-and-white pup and allow him to visit her regularly.

Wags gave Simone a wet, loving lick on the chin, softening her even more.

"All right," she finally said. "He can stay. But only until you find another place. I have no idea how Woofer is going to feel about having him here, and I could be making a big mistake."

"You said Woofer doesn't even know that he's a dog," Mike said. "He thinks he's human. And all kids need a pet. Woofer will probably love having this little guy to pal around with."

"I hope so."

Mike *knew* so. Finding Wags hadn't been an accident. Fate had stepped in to give him and Simone another helping hand.

"Where are his things?" Simone asked.

"His *things?*"

"You know, puppy food, toys…"

Simone's pretty brown eyes grew large and luminous. "All you brought is a puppy and an empty cardboard box?"

Oops. He'd been in such a hurry to bring Wags to Simone that he hadn't thought about her not having everything the puppy would need. Last night, he'd knotted up an old sock for him to chew on, although he'd left it at home. And then he'd fed him some leftover steak that had been chopped up. This morning, he'd given Wags scrambled eggs and bacon. So it wasn't as if he'd neglected to take care of him. But a shopping trip was definitely in order.

He could do it on his own, but maybe it would be in his best interests to feign ignorance. "I'll be happy to purchase whatever he needs, but you'd better come with me. I'm not sure what to buy."

She looked at him in disbelief, and he suspected she might decline to go with him.

But then again, fate seemed to be working in his favor when she handed Wags back to him. "All right. You take the puppy to the car and I'll meet you there."

"What are you going to do?"

"I need to go to the bathroom and grab my purse."

"Your purse is in the bathroom?"

She shot him a frown that suggested she didn't find his joke funny. "Just give me a minute, will you?"

Sure. He'd give her all the time she needed.

At thirty-two, he was ready to get married. And if it took her a bit longer to get used to the idea, then so be it.

Her arguments would soon go by the wayside.

So what if she was older than he was? Or if she wasn't used to big, happy families?

And so what if she wasn't ready to settle down?

Mike was a focused competitor and believed that there wasn't anything he couldn't do or have—once he set his mind to it.

And he'd set his mind—and his heart—on Simone.

Chapter Two

Simone handed little Wags back to Mike. She hoped and prayed he wouldn't ask to use her bathroom before she got rid of the testing apparatus. If he did, she'd have to race him there.

She crossed her arms and waited for him to head for his Jeep, yet he merely stood in the living room, studying her with expressive green eyes and a dimpled grin.

"I really appreciate this," he said.

She supposed he did, but she wasn't keen on taking care of Wags for him, no matter how cute either Mike or the puppy was.

Nor was she up for a shopping trip.

But agreeing to go with him seemed to be the quickest way to get him out of her house. And the sooner he went outside, the better.

"I won't be long," she said. "You can even go out to the car and start the engine, if you'd like to."

"That's all right. I'll just wait for you here." Mike glanced at Wags. "We don't mind, do we, buddy?"

The longer her one-night lover remained in her house, the more uneasy she became.

She doubted that he suspected anything, though.

How could he?

"Okay," she finally said. Then she turned and hurried to the bathroom, where she locked herself inside.

With her secret safe for the time being, she rested her back against the door and blew out a ragged sigh. Then, feeling only slightly relieved, she quickly scooped up the plastic apparatus that still displayed evidence of the baby they'd created and shoved it into the back of the cupboard, behind a stack of towels.

As soon as she returned home, and Mike was no longer around, she would double-bag the test kit in two plastic grocery sacks and throw it away.

Of course, she'd have to level with him sometime and tell him she was pregnant, but she was still processing the news herself.

So, some other day, when the time was right, she'd let him know that it was her problem, not his. And that she wouldn't need anything from him. She would also tell him she'd decided to give up the baby for adoption, which was the best thing she could do for everyone involved, especially her child.

Adoption was the decision she'd wished her mother had made when she'd been pregnant with Simone. Instead, her mom had botched up the whole mother/daughter thing, something that continued to plague them both to this day.

Simone flushed the toilet, just to make Mike think she'd had the usual reasons for locking herself in the bathroom, then washed her hands and dried them on a white, fluffy towel reserved for guests.

Not that she and Woofer had many of them.

Dr. Ella Wilder stopped by sometimes. So did Isobel Suarez, the hospital social worker who'd become a friend.

Of course, Mike was here now—and waiting for her.

She looked in the mirror, caught the frumpy, pale image looking back at her.

Her hair, which had been put into a just-hanging-out-at-home ponytail earlier, had come loose. And she wasn't wearing any makeup whatsoever.

Dressed in her favorite pair of well-worn jeans and a Rosie the Riveter T-shirt, she was a mind-boggling contrast to the chic, sexy woman who'd invited Mike into her house and into her bed five weeks ago.

But she didn't feel like putting on makeup or a happy face. Nor did she want to draw attention to herself in a feminine sense.

After all, look what had happened when she'd dressed up for that cocktail party and had pretended to be someone she wasn't.

But she couldn't very well go out looking like a total frump, although she wouldn't change her clothes. How could she when she wore a shirt with Rosie the Riveter rolling up a sleeve and proclaiming, "We can do it!"

So trying to draw upon Rosie's confidence and determination, she removed the rubber band and ran a brush through her hair, leaving it down. Then she dug into her makeup drawer and pulled out a tube of lipstick. But after taking off the cap, she paused.

She really didn't want Mike to think she was getting dolled up for his benefit. Of course, the sexy paramedic didn't need that kind of encouragement.

The first time he'd come on to her—more than a year ago—had been in the hospital doctors' lounge, where she'd been pouring herself a cup of overbrewed coffee. She was wearing a pair of blue scrubs and was close to finishing up a long, grueling twelve-hour shift.

"Hey," he'd said. "I've got tickets to a concert at the Stardust Theater on Thursday. And I've asked around. We're both off that night."

She'd caught him looking at her several times in the past, and the intensity in his gaze had always spiked her pulse. Mike O'Rourke was a handsome man, and any woman would be flattered to know she'd caught his eye.

But Simone hadn't expected his interest in her to take a romantic turn, and her senses had reeled.

"I…uh…I've already got plans," she'd lied, scrambling to come up with an excuse.

And she'd been putting him off ever since, even though he told her he was prepared to wait until she was ready to give "them" a try.

He'd never been pushy, but now that they'd slept together, his determination seemed to have grown stronger.

So she re-capped the lipstick without using it and put it away. Then she slid the bathroom drawer shut and headed to her bedroom for her purse and a light sweater—just in case. The New England weather was always a bit unpredictable in April, although the past few days had been remarkably pleasant.

When she returned to the living room, Mike was standing by the door, ready to go.

He held Wags in the crook of his arm and opened the door for her with his free hand. Then he waited on the sidewalk while she made sure Woofer had fresh water and locked up the house.

"Where do you suggest we go to find dog supplies?" he asked.

"There's a pet store on Lexington, across from Prudy's Menu. It's called Tails a Waggin', and they'll have everything we'll need."

"All right. I know where that is." He opened the passenger door of his Jeep Wrangler, and after she climbed into the seat, he handed Wags to her. "He hates that box if he's awake. Why don't you hold him."

Simone took the squirming pup. She had to admit, it was a cute little thing. But she needed another dog around the house like she needed a hole in the head, and she couldn't help wondering what she'd gotten herself into.

Wasn't her life going to be complicated enough for the next seven or eight months?

"Thanks for coming with me," he said. "I don't want to forget anything."

"No problem," she said, although she wasn't being entirely truthful.

She really wasn't in the mood to go anywhere. Not when she had a stack of laundry to do at home. She'd also planned to clean out the refrigerator and wash the windows, chores she saved for her day off. And she'd told Woofer she would take him for a long walk this afternoon.

Not that the dog would hold her to it, she supposed. But some things easily became habits that were hard to break.

And speaking of habits, she couldn't even imagine

the effect a new puppy was going to have on her normal routine.

Of course, a baby would really shake things up.

Thank goodness she knew better than to open herself up to that.

Mike backed his Jeep out of Simone's driveway and drove through Riverdale, an older part of town, where the houses near the river had been built in the 1940s. With only a few exceptions, the yards and structures had been kept up throughout the years.

"I've always liked this neighborhood," he said, thinking it had a Norman Rockwell appeal.

"Me, too." Simone glanced out the window, as though appreciating the maples, sycamores and the occasional hemlock that shaded the sidewalks and the street on which she lived.

When Mike and his brothers were in high school, they'd worked summers for their uncle, who was a building contractor. As a result, each of the boys could do just about anything—electrical, plumbing, drywall, painting—skills that could turn an old house into something special.

A lot of people might prefer to buy newer homes, but Mike was drawn to the quaint, nostalgic ambience of this particular neighborhood. In fact, he'd told his Realtor that he was looking for a fixer-upper but wouldn't mind purchasing anything in Riverdale, should one of the properties become available.

"Did you have to do a lot of work after you moved in?" he asked, thinking about the cozy, two-bedroom brick structure she'd purchased.

"Yes, but it was actually fun to roll up my sleeves and watch things change before my eyes. I even took some of those home-improvement classes they offer at Hadley's Hardware Store. I couldn't afford to do everything at once, but I started by working on one room at a time. The first thing I did was to tear up the carpeting and refinish the original hardwood flooring. Then I painted."

Overall, he had to say he liked what she'd done to the place, although his focus had been on more than beige walls and white crown molding the night he'd taken her home.

In fact, as they'd left the cocktail party, he'd stolen a kiss while the two of them stood next to his Jeep, and his hormones hadn't given him or his brain cells a free moment until dawn.

He'd known their lovemaking would be good, but it had been better than either of them could have imagined, and they'd awakened like a pair of spoons, completely spent and sated.

Yet one night hadn't been enough.

He slid a sidelong glance across the seat and saw that she was staring straight ahead and biting her bottom lip. Then she glanced at him, lips parting.

Had her thoughts gone in a sexual direction, too? Was she thinking about the pleasure they'd given each other in the antique bed in her candlelit room?

He suspected so, because her words seemed to have dissipated in the cab of the Jeep.

But he didn't let the silence get to him. "I told Karen, Leif's sister, that I'd be interested in buying something in this part of town, especially if it needed some work."

She tucked a strand of hair behind her ear. "I'll keep

my eyes and ears open. Mark Griffith, who lives with his wife and son on Ash, might have to be transferred to another office out of state. If so, he might be interested in selling."

"That would work out great for me." Since Simone didn't comment either way about the possibility of them being neighbors, he let it drop.

Minutes later, he pulled the Jeep into a parking spot on Lexington, two spaces down from the pet shop, and turned off the ignition.

"How'd you know about this place?" he asked.

"Originally, Ella Wilder mentioned it to me."

"She has animals?"

"Yes, a cat named Molly. She found the poor little thing injured and lying on the side of the road. A lot of people might have put her to sleep since she lost a leg, but Ella nursed her back to health."

Mike never figured the young orthopedic surgeon as an animal lover, but then again, he hadn't suspected Simone to be one, either. Not until he'd seen her with Woofer.

"One day, after shopping, I stopped at Prudy's Menu to place a take-home order, and I noticed it across the street. Ella had said it was a mom-and-pop–type store and that it could almost be entertaining at times. So I decided to check it out. And that's the day I met Woofer."

"You've gotta be kidding. I thought pet stores only sold animals with pedigrees."

"Actually, the Baxters allow several different pet-rescue organizations to hold adoption days at the store on weekends. And that's exactly what was going on the first time I stopped in to visit."

"Wait a minute." Mike slid her a crooked grin. "You

mean that you make a point of visiting the pet store even when you don't have anything to buy?"

"Yes, I do that every once in a while. Millie and Fred Baxter are nice people. I first met them a year or so ago when Fred was brought into the E.R. after suffering chest pains."

"Oh, yeah?"

Simone had always told him that she tried not to get attached to her patients, which is why she enjoyed working in the E.R. Most of the patients were just passing through. But obviously, she got attached to some of them.

"Fred had suffered a major heart attack," she said.

"Obviously, he pulled through."

Simone nodded. "Millie was trying to be tough for his sake, but I could see the fear in her eyes. They were pretty young to be going through something like that, and for some reason, I was drawn to her. So when I was off duty that evening, I picked up a cup of coffee in the doctors' lounge, then offered it to her. I sat with her for a few minutes, and we started chatting."

Mike had seen Simone with her patients, and while she was good to all of them when they were in her care, she was able to detach when they were either admitted or discharged.

And she didn't normally spend her free time visiting with them.

"What was so special about Millie?" he asked. There had to have been something that appealed to Simone, and he was curious to know what it was. To know what drew her to certain people.

Simone shrugged, then focused her attention on the

puppy in her lap, her thoughts appearing to drift somewhere else.

When she glanced up, her gaze snagged his, tugging at his heart in that way only Simone could do. "I'm really not a romantic person, so you'll probably think this is weird coming from me, but I think Fred and Millie are soul mates—if there is such a thing."

There was. Mike suspected he and Simone were, too, but she hadn't quite figured it out yet.

"Anyway," Simone continued, "Millie was worried about losing Fred, which was understandable. But she mentioned they'd been trying to…" Simone paused and glanced out the passenger side of the window, as though distracted and drifting off topic.

"Trying to *what?*" Mike asked, steering her back to the conversation they'd been having.

She cleared her throat. "They'd been trying to have a baby for years and had finally given up. In vitro and other expensive fertility treatments are out of the question, since they're new business owners and have poured their savings into the store. They'd just started the adoption process when Fred was brought into the E.R. However, Millie realized that his heart condition might make it more difficult for them to adopt."

Again, Simone glanced out into the distance, but Mike could see the cogs turning, her mind drifting, and he wished she'd share those thoughts with him.

He couldn't imagine his future without kids. He adored his nieces and nephews and looked forward to the day he could give them a couple of cousins to play with.

She obviously felt badly that Millie couldn't have the family she'd dreamed of. Maybe that was because

Simone harbored some secret maternal urges, too. And if so, that would play right into Mike's hands.

Unless, of course, Simone had reason to believe that she couldn't have children. Maybe that's why she took such a strong stance against marriage or even a relationship.

"Adopting a child is a good option," Mike said, just in case he'd touched on a sore subject. He wanted her to know that he'd be okay if she was infertile—disappointed, but okay. "And there's always a need for good foster parents. So even if a person can't have kids of their own, there are plenty of opportunities to be parents."

"Yes, you're right." Her voice came out soft, burdened. "Millie's the kind of woman who would make a great mother. And if I were a kid, I would have loved to have someone like her adopt me."

One night at the hospital, he'd mentioned that he came from a big family and that he hoped to have a few children of his own someday. She admitted to being an only child and said she wasn't big on kids.

But that couldn't be true. She was terrific with the pediatric patients who came in to the E.R.

"You know," Mike said, "not being able to have children wouldn't be the end of the world."

"You're right. And honestly, Millie was far more concerned about losing Fred than her chance at adopting a baby. She loves him more than anything in the world and is glad to have him for as long as possible. She's also resigned to the fact that their pets will be the only children they have." Simone unhooked her seat belt, handed Wags to Mike and reached for the door handle. "Come on, I'll introduce you to one of the nicest couples in Walnut River."

* * *

Millie Baxter, a tall, slender blonde in her late thirties, broke into a smile that lit up the room when she spotted Simone enter the pet shop.

"Well, if it isn't my favorite nurse." She left her position near the cash register and greeted Simone at the door with a warm hug.

The Baxters tried hard to remember the names of not only their customers, but also their customers' pets, but they didn't offer hugs to just anyone.

"Where's Woofer?" Millie asked.

"He's at home and not all that happy about it. But he'd really be pouting if he knew where I was. He loves coming here with me to shop, although part of the reason is because of those meaty treats you always give him." Simone turned to Mike and introduced him to Millie, calling him her friend and mentioning that he was a paramedic.

"And who is this sweet little guy?" Millie asked, zeroing in on the puppy in Mike's arms.

"His name is Wags," Mike said, "and he's going to stay with Simone until I find another place to live."

"I'll bet Woofer loves *you*," Millie said to the dog.

"They haven't met yet," Simone said. "And I'm not sure how Woofer is going to feel about sharing my time or having a houseguest."

"Just take it slow and easy when you introduce them. There's always a bit of an adjustment period, but I'm sure they'll be the best of friends before you know it." Millie looked at Mike. "Would you like me to hold Wags for you while you shop?"

"Thanks. I have a feeling we'll be needing both

hands." Mike passed the puppy to Millie. "So, if you'll excuse me, I'd better get a cart."

"Where's Fred?" Simone asked. She hoped he was feeling okay and hadn't stayed home.

"Helen Walters purchased a new aquarium for her nephew, so he drove over to the boy's house to help them set it up. He's been gone quite a while, so I expect him back soon."

The Baxters were very generous with their time and their expertise, so going the extra mile wasn't surprising.

"That was sweet of Fred to help."

"Aw, you know how Fred is." Millie smiled, eyes crinkling. "If there's anything he likes more than animals it's kids."

"Okay," Mike said upon his return with a cart. "Where do we find the dog supplies?"

"They're on aisle one." Simone pointed to the right. "I'll show you."

As they strode through the small but well-stocked and -organized shop, Simone pointed to the basset hound snoozing on a blue pad by the cash register. She noticed that he was wearing the usual bandanna around his neck. It was red this time, although the color and print usually varied from day to day.

"That's Popeye Baxter," Simone told Mike. "He comes to work with Fred and Millie each day and is practically a fixture around here."

"Lucky dog."

"Yes, he certainly is. The Baxters own quite a few pets." All of which they referred to as "the kids."

"Are the other animals here at the store?"

"Most of them are. Tina the cat is usually playing on

a carpet-covered climbing structure in the kitty section. And Herb the parrot is perched in the bird aisle."

Mike scanned the interior of the pet store. "I can see why you like to stop in and visit."

"Can you?" she asked. She'd always thought animal lovers were a bit…over the top. But that was until she met the Baxters—and adopted Woofer. The big, goofy dog had really grown on her. She suspected that was because she and the mutt had a lot in common.

"Honey," a man's voice rang out. "I'm back."

"That's Fred." Simone nodded to the short, heavyset man who'd entered the store through the back door. "I'll introduce you after we finish stocking up on supplies."

Ten minutes later, they'd filled the cart with a doggie bed, chew toys, puppy food, a pet carrier, leash and collar.

"Hey, wait." Mike threw in a bulky piece of knotted rope and a rawhide bone. "We don't want Woofer feeling left out."

She figured the toys would all become community property eventually. "You don't need to worry about Woofer."

"Maybe not, but my sister Kari just had her second baby—a boy. And she bought a doll and a toy stroller for his big sister. She didn't want her little girl to be jealous of the new baby."

See? Simone knew nothing about that sort of thing, which was another reason she would make a lousy mother, if given the chance.

"You know," Mike said as they approached the checkout counter, "speaking of kids, this kind of feels like we're preparing a doggie nursery."

The hint of a chuckle tickled the tone of his voice,

but Simone didn't find anything warm or amusing in the words.

They *weren't* co–dog owners.

And there wasn't anything parental about their relationship, even though a child they'd created was growing in Simone's womb.

A sense of uneasiness settled over her as she thought of giving up the baby. But the child deserved a loving home with two parents, a couple who would lovingly prepare a nursery in anticipation of the child they'd always wanted. And she tamped down the momentary discomfort.

Simone glanced at Millie and recognized a soulful longing that whisked across her face, a momentary stab of grief.

It wasn't likely that Millie and Fred would ever have the chance to decorate a nursery. And the shame of it all was that they'd make great parents. If given the opportunity, they'd welcome a new baby…

Simone's musing took an interesting turn.

Maybe Fred and Millie would want her baby.

Wouldn't it be easier to give the child to people she knew? A couple she trusted?

It was certainly something to consider. And she hoped that Mike would see the wisdom in it—when the time came to tell him that during their one night together they conceived a baby.

She sure hoped he wouldn't give her a hard time about the decision she'd made.

Still, her tummy tossed and turned.

What if Mike didn't agree? What if he didn't let up on her and tried to push her into something she knew was wrong—at least, for her?

"That will be a hundred and twenty-seven dollars and sixteen cents," Millie said, drawing Simone from her musing.

Mike whipped out his credit card in a blur. Or so it seemed.

Simone blinked, feeling a bit dizzy and light-headed.

Whew. All she needed to do was to pass out. The dedicated paramedic and the dutiful suitor in Mike would have a field day with that.

Uh-oh.

A buzz filled her ears, and she reached for Mike's arm, felt the bulge of muscle tense.

He turned and caught her eye, his smile morphing into a frown. "What's the matter?"

"I…" Damn. She didn't want to tell him. But if she didn't, he was going to figure it out all by himself. "I think I'm going to…"

Her knees buckled before she could finish the thought.

Chapter Three

Mike caught Simone in his arms just before she crumpled to the pet-shop floor.

As much as he wanted to hold her close, to cling to the citrusy scent of her bath soap and shampoo, he gently laid her down and knelt beside her. He might be medically trained and competent in an emergency, but he wasn't at all prepared for Simone's collapse.

"Oh my gosh," Millie said, hurrying around the counter to see what was going on. "Is she okay? What happened?"

Mike didn't know for sure. "I think she fainted."

Simone's vulnerability damn near sent him reeling, and he took her hand, checking her pulse while assessing her respiration. He placed a hand on her forehead to gauge her temperature and found it cool, so she didn't have a fever.

Her lashes, dark and lush against the skin that had gone pale, fluttered ever so slightly.

"Fred!" Millie called. "Come quick!"

Simone lifted her lids, blinking them a couple of times until her eyes searched Mike's face, as though she was trying to focus.

When she tried to sit up, he stopped her. "Just lie still for a minute or two."

"Okay." She drew in a shaky breath, then slowly blew it out.

"How are you feeling?" Mike ran his knuckles along her cheek—God, he'd missed touching her.

"A little light-headed and buzzy, but nothing hurts."

Again, she began to fold up into a sit. And this time, he placed his hands on her shoulders and gently held her down. "I'm calling the shots, and you need to lie still a little longer."

She offered him a wry smile. "I thought paramedics were supposed to yield to the nursing staff."

"Yeah, well, not when the nurse is incapacitated." He tried to shrug off his concern, but couldn't. What the hell had happened? And why?

Damn. He wanted to do so much more than tell her to stay put and to remain quiet, but she was conscious. And he couldn't find any of her vitals out of whack. So he relied on his training to tell him she was okay when his heart was telling him to call 911 and ask for backup.

Deciding upon a compromise, he said, "As soon as you feel up to moving, I'll take you to the hospital and get you checked out."

"No, that's not necessary. I'll be okay." She closed

her eyes, but only for a moment. "This isn't serious, Mike. Besides, it was my own fault."

"What do you mean?"

"I haven't eaten anything since yesterday at lunch, and I really should have grabbed a snack on our way out the door."

He hoped she wasn't dieting; she didn't need to lose weight. She was in *great* shape. And even if she *could* stand to lose a couple of pounds, she ought to know that starvation wasn't the way to go.

"I got a little light-headed and—" she shrugged her shoulders "—I passed out."

She could say *that* again.

He watched the color slowly creep back into her face. "Why haven't you been eating?"

"I was tired when I got home from work last night and decided to stretch out on the sofa and watch a little television before fixing dinner. The next thing I knew, it was morning." She slowly sat up and leaned her back against the counter. "And when I woke up, I... Well, I just got busy. That's all."

And then he'd dragged her shopping for pet supplies. Great.

By this time, Fred Baxter came running to their side, his breathing heavy and more labored than a short, indoor jog should have caused. "Oh my goodness! *Simone.* What happened?"

"I fainted," she said. "I'm sure it was caused by low blood sugar."

"I've got some orange juice in the back room," Millie said. "And a granola bar."

"That would help." Simone slowly sat up, then ran a hand through her hair. "Thank you."

As Millie hurried through the store, Mike said, "You're going to need to eat more than juice and a snack. I'll take you across the street to the deli so you can order lunch."

And for once, when it came to Simone, he wasn't going to sit back and let her call the shots.

Minutes after Fred had loaded their purchases into Mike's Jeep and returned the key, Simone allowed Mike to lead her across the street to Prudy's Menu. The small bakery/deli specialized in scrumptious desserts, gourmet coffees and teas, as well as homemade breads, soups and sandwiches.

They sat at one of the green bistro tables that graced the street-front patio of the eatery. An umbrella shaded them and their place settings from the dappled sunlight that filtered through the leaves of several old maples that grew along Lexington Avenue.

The waitress had just given them water and taken their orders.

"Are you feeling better now?" Mike asked.

"I'm still a little shaky, but it's passing." Simone offered him a smile she hoped was convincing.

She wasn't used to being coddled or taken care of. Even as a kid, when she'd actually been sick, she'd had to fend for herself. So she'd gotten accustomed to being alone when she was under the weather and, to be honest, actually preferred it that way. For a woman who dispensed endless doses of TLC for a living, she was uneasy being on the receiving end.

Of course, now that she'd had a granola bar to eat and some juice to sip, she was almost back to normal—at least, physically. Emotionally, not so much. The news of her pregnancy was still a little unsettling.

Giving the baby up might not be easy, but it would be for the best.

"Are you too cold?" he asked. "Or too warm? We can go back inside if you'd be more comfortable."

She reached across the table and placed her hand over the top of his. "I'm *fine*. And I'll be even better when the waitress brings my soup. Besides, we have to sit outside because of Wags."

"You're right, but I'll bet Millie and Fred would have watched the puppy for us."

Simone peered under the table, where Wags was tethered to a chair leg by a new red collar and leash. He was so content to be greedily chomping on a little rawhide bone that he didn't even glance up at her. "Look how happy he is."

Mike's gaze remained on her. "If it gets too warm for you out here, if the sun is too bright, let me know and I'll take him across the street so we can go inside."

"The temperature is perfect. And besides, the fresh air will help clear my head." She offered him another don't-worry-about-me smile, then scanned the small patio, where only one other group of diners—an elderly man and two women—sat.

There hadn't been many people wanting to eat outdoors during the winter months, so it was nice to see the weather changing. And while she knew a cold spell could still strike at any time, she preferred to think that spring was here to stay.

Apparently, Belle, Prudy's daughter who was now running the eatery, agreed, because there were several pots of red geraniums gracing the patio that hadn't been there the last time Simone had stopped in for a bite to eat.

When the waitress brought their lunch—a turkey sandwich and vegetable soup for her and a pastrami on rye for Mike—Simone dug in.

The fainting spell was probably a combination of pregnancy hormones as well as a low blood sugar level from not eating, but she would talk to the doctor to make sure. There was no reason to take any unnecessary chances or to jeopardize the baby's health. From now on, she would put the child's best interests above her own.

Simone didn't need a psychiatric evaluation to tell her the baby would be much better off with another mom. She'd wished a hundred times over that her mother would have had the courage to do the right thing when faced with an unwanted, unplanned pregnancy. Susan Garner would have done herself and Simone a huge favor by signing over maternal rights at birth, but that hadn't happened.

And now, ironically, Simone was faced with the same decision. And while that decision might have come quickly, it wasn't being made easily.

Would the baby look like Mike, with his black hair and green eyes? Or would it look more like her?

She could hardly imagine.

Had her mother been faced with those same questions when she'd been pregnant?

Maybe even more so, under the circumstances. And

she suspected that when handed a baby who favored her father, Susan Garner had recoiled emotionally.

Genetics could be a real bitch sometimes.

When Simone had taken her second bite of the sandwich, she glanced up to catch Mike studying her. His hair, as black as a young raven's wing, was spiked in a style that suited him. And his eyes, as green as a blade of new grass, were intense and quick.

He was of medium height, but there was nothing average or run-of-the-mill about him.

Their gazes locked, as they sometimes did, with a bond of friendship and professional respect.

So there was a bit of sexual attraction, too. But she knew better than to latch onto something as fleeting as that and glanced back at her food.

"Maybe you ought to see your doctor and have your glucose level checked," he said.

"Don't worry. Now that I'm eating, I feel much better."

"Okay, but promise me you'll make an appointment with the doctor anyway."

Simone placed her half-eaten sandwich on the plate, then picked up her soupspoon. "All right. I'll do that as soon as I get home."

It was a promise she meant to keep, but she wouldn't call Dr. Grayson, her general practitioner. Instead, she would contact Dr. Kipper's office and schedule her first obstetrical appointment.

Of course, at thirty-seven, it was a little embarrassing to be unmarried and expecting a baby, but at least something good would come of it—especially if she could set up a private adoption with Millie and Fred.

Yes, she understood that Fred had some serious

health issues, but he was a wonderful man. Her baby would be lucky to have a daddy like him.

"Okay," Mike said, "you're probably right."

She glanced up from her nearly empty bowl, knowing that she hadn't been thinking out loud, but having the strangest feeling that he'd been privy to her musing. "Right about what?"

"You're wolfing down your food as though you hadn't eaten in ages."

"I told you that I hadn't. Didn't you believe me?"

"You've never lied to me, so I guess I have no reason not to."

Would his worry increase if he knew she was pregnant?

Once Mike had implied that she would make the perfect wife. And he'd made no secret that he was ready to settle down and start a family.

She sure hoped he wouldn't give her a hard time about the decision she'd made. Surely he'd see the wisdom in it.

And if he didn't?

She could recite a list of reasons why it was the perfect decision—for both of them.

First, there was the age difference. And she wasn't just talking chronologically. Simone had always been older than her years, even as a child; she'd had to be.

Secondly, his upbringing had been so completely different from hers that the two of them had very little in common. Mike had tons of stories he could relate about his childhood, memories that always brought a smile to his face. And on the other hand…well, hers were better left unsaid.

In addition, Mike had been born into a big, happy

family. And Simone—an only child and a loner by nature—wasn't comfortable in a crowd, especially when there were expectations of intimacy.

The one and only serious boyfriend she'd had in college had referred to her as an ice queen.

At the time, she'd laughed it off, but the words had hurt since they'd held a ring of truth. And while she preferred to think of herself as having intimacy issues, it hadn't taken a major in psychology to connect the dots and realize that it was a miracle she'd become the woman she was.

So what if she'd avoided having a relationship with another man after that?

She might not be able to pin her hopes and dreams on having a typical home and family, but she was happy with herself—and with her life.

Eventually, Mike would realize that she'd done them both a favor by refusing to let him get tied down with a woman he would soon grow unhappy with.

She looked up from her meal, saw him relishing his pastrami on rye as though he didn't have a problem in the world.

And he didn't.

The pregnancy dilemma and possible solutions were hers.

Still, a wave of nausea rolled across her stomach, something that she believed had more of an emotional cause than hormonal.

She pushed her empty soup bowl aside.

What if Mike didn't agree with her decision to put the baby up for adoption? What if he didn't let up on her about wanting some kind of commitment?

She didn't want to jeopardize her friendship with Mike; she truly liked the handsome paramedic.

But if worst came to worst, she would be forced to shut him out of her life—permanently.

As Simone led Mike along the sidewalk to her front door, Woofer howled at the side gate, welcoming her home.

"Hey, buddy," Mike said. "We've got a surprise for you."

"It'll be a surprise, all right." Simone glanced at the puppy in her arms. "I'm not sure how he's going to feel about having Wags as a houseguest."

"He'll adjust," Mike said.

Simone let them into the house, then went to the back door to greet Woofer.

Mike hadn't given it much thought before, but he now realized that if the big dog didn't take to the puppy, he'd be in a bind. Of course, Woofer didn't seem to have a mean bone in his body, so maybe he was being overly concerned.

He took a seat on the sofa and waited for Simone to return. He could hear the click of the lock as she opened the door and let in the dog.

"Ar-oof, ar-oof." Woofer's tail thumped against something in the kitchen, and his claws scratched against the floor.

Since Simone didn't immediately return, Mike figured she was trying to calm Woofer down in the other room before allowing him into the front of the house.

Maybe bringing the puppy here hadn't been such a good idea after all.

Mike looked at Wags and whispered, "If she wouldn't have fainted earlier this morning, I wouldn't feel so uneasy about this now."

Of course, Simone had seemed fine during lunch and on the way back home.

Moments later, Simone led Woofer into the living room, and when the happy-go-lucky mutt spotted Mike, he padded across the hardwood floor to greet him. But he froze in his tracks the moment he saw the puppy and made a growl-like grunt.

Mike put Wags on the floor, and the pup began to check out his surroundings, oblivious to Woofer. That is, until Woofer decided to investigate the new arrival.

After ten minutes, several barks, a few whines and a whole lot of sniffing, the dogs began to tolerate each other.

"What do you think?" Mike asked.

"I think I need to have my head examined for agreeing to look after Wags. These two are going to need a human chaperone."

"Our work schedules ought to overlap some, so I can stop by and look after them when you're not home. At least, some of the time. I have to leave for work pretty soon, but since your shift doesn't start until tomorrow, it ought to be okay."

For a moment, she seemed to ponder his suggestion to share the burden of both dogs, then she shrugged. "Let's just take things one day at a time. I'll take the first watch this evening. And we'll see how it goes."

"Okay."

While the dogs continued to check each other out, the humans seemed to be tiptoeing around their thoughts and feelings. At least, Mike was.

Simone had once said that she couldn't figure out what a guy like him saw in her. But the answer was a no-brainer to Mike.

He'd witnessed the compassion that drove her and made her one of the best nurses on staff at Walnut River General. And he'd seen the emotion that pooled under her cool surface.

No, there weren't many women like Simone Garner in this world, and the rest seemed to fall short, at least in Mike's eyes.

He glanced at his watch. "I guess I'd better take off. I really appreciate this."

"You're going to definitely owe me a huge favor after this." Her eyes, as warm and sweet as a melted puddle of milk chocolate, glistened.

"You're right." And he'd be happy to come up with ways to repay her, although he figured she still needed more time. So he stood and let her walk him to the front door.

"How about a thank-you dinner at Rafael's on Saturday night?" he asked. "Maybe you can wear that little black dress that looked dynamite on you."

She crossed her arms. "I'm afraid that dress and Rafael's would be a little too romantic for me."

"Listen." Mike placed his index finger under her chin and tilted her face to his. "I'm not sure why you're fighting your feelings for me."

"We've talked about this several times, and if you think about it, you'll realize my answers have always been consistent."

"Well, you're *not* too old for me. And I have no problem if we don't socialize very much. I've learned what a nice quiet evening at home can be like, and you won't find any argument from me." He tossed her a boyish grin. "I'd agree to another sleepover anytime."

She shifted her weight to one foot, and her cheeks flushed. An emotional reaction to either the memory or the reminder, he suspected.

"As nice as it was, it was a one-night stand," she said.

"No way, honey. I'm not sure how many of those you've had, but I can tell you from experience that first-time lovers don't get in tune with each other's bodies that way."

"Okay, I admit it was good. Great, even. But a relationship between us will never work. I'm not family material, and you grew up like one of the Waltons."

So Mike was one of five kids, and Simone didn't have siblings. He couldn't see a problem in that. Couples compromised all the time, learning to respect each other's differences. Hell, his father had been raised Catholic, and his mom had been Protestant through and through. They hadn't let it stand in their way, so he couldn't buy *that* excuse.

"Do you think about it at all?" he asked. "The night we spent together?"

She didn't answer, but he saw the struggle in her eyes. The fight between heart and mind. At least, he could swear that's what he kept seeing in her. Normally, he knew how to cut bait and run when a woman wasn't interested.

But his gut told him Simone was different. She wasn't being coy or shy. Neither was she playing games.

She wanted him as badly as he wanted her. And there was only one reason she'd fight the feeling.

"Someone in the past hurt you, Simone." His words seemed to strike some tender spot in her heart—God, he sure hoped they had, that he'd finally gotten to the bottom of whatever was standing between them.

As he studied her troubled expression, he realized his words had hit the mark.

"I'm not going to pry and dig for the truth," he added. "But I can see it in your eyes. You're afraid to let go and love me. But the feelings are there, brewing under the surface."

"That's not love, it's lust," she said, her voice husky with it.

"There's that, too." He was tempted to kiss her, long and deep and thorough, but he wasn't at all ready to start something he couldn't finish. Not when he had a shift starting soon. "But I'm serious about giving you the time you need."

Then he reached for the doorknob to let himself out.

"You're right," she finally admitted.

He turned, his gaze snagging hers. "Right about what?"

"About me being hurt in the past, about me being afraid to get close to people. But those scars are deep and permanent."

"Then you can't blame me for wanting to be the guy who makes them disappear."

They stood like that for a while, a man and a woman teetering on an emotional precipice that someone else had created.

He was sorely tempted to brush a kiss across her lips, to taunt her with memories of the sexual pleasure they'd found in each other's arms more than a month ago. But instead, he kissed her forehead, much like his mother used to do to him and his siblings when they'd scraped an elbow or stubbed a toe.

"I'll call you in the morning," he said before letting himself out and closing the door behind him.

Time, he figured, was his best ally. He knew her scars were deep. He just hoped they weren't as permanent as she wanted him to believe.

Chapter Four

Woofer found his new playmate entertaining, but when he grew tired of the puppy's games and wanted to rest, little Wags was still going strong.

There'd been a few growls and yips and whines at first, but as the day wore on, the dogs grew more and more comfortable with each other.

So far, so good, Simone thought as she locked up the house and turned off the porch light.

Woofer usually slept in her bedroom each night, but since Wags wasn't housebroken yet, she decided to put them both in the kitchen. One of the purchases Mike had made was a portable gate Millie Baxter had said might come in handy for separating the two, if it became necessary, and Simone had put it to good use several times.

Neither Wags nor Woofer was happy about being contained, and she hoped they would adjust soon.

After taking a nice long shower, she put on a flannel nightgown and pulled down the covers to her bed. The faint scent of laundry detergent and fabric softener reminded her the sheets were clean and fresh.

As she climbed onto the mattress and fluffed her pillow, it was the first real moment she'd had to relax all day, the first time she'd had a chance to ponder something other than dogs.

And that something was Mike.

Do you ever think about the night we spent together? he'd asked.

Of course she did. How could she not?

She'd never let down her defenses like that before. But there were several reasons she had.

She'd felt unusually pretty the night of Dr. Wilder's cocktail party.

Dressed in a sexy dress and heels while holding the flute of bubbly had also made her feel elegant and sophisticated—a nice change for a woman who spent her workday wearing scrubs and her time off in an oversize shirt and a pair of comfy sweats or well-worn jeans.

As luck would have it, the conscientious waiter kept refilling her glass until she'd had a mind-numbing buzz, which had made the night seem surreal.

And as enchanting as a fairy tale.

Just seeing the way Mike had looked at her was enough to make her lose her head and pretend to be someone else.

And as he'd taken her hand and led her from the party and out of Peter's house, she'd wondered if the night air would have the same effect on her as the clock striking midnight had on Cinderella.

But it hadn't.

Overhead, the wintry sky was adorned with a million twinkling stars. And all around them, crystal flakes glistened on the banks of fresh-fallen snow.

When they'd reached Mike's Jeep, he'd drawn her into his embrace. Then he'd tilted her chin and lowered his mouth to hers. She should have stopped it right there, but her pulse and her hormones had been pumping like a runaway steam engine, and she'd been lost in the magic of the heated moment.

The first tentative touch of his lips to hers had quickly intensified into a mind-spinning, knee-weakening kiss.

If she closed her eyes, she could imagine it still, the way his tongue had swept into her mouth, stealing her senses and making her ache for more.

Her physical reaction, which had bordered on wild and wicked, at least for someone as staid and conservative as she was, had merely been a result of lust and alcohol.

Still, whether she liked admitting it or not, something deep inside her was moved by Mike's charm and flattered by his crush on her. So when he'd driven her home, she'd thrown caution to the wind and continued to play the role of a princess at the ball. And for the next few hours, she'd pretended to be a woman who always wore her hair swept up in a classic twist, someone who actually belonged in a sexy dress and spiked heels.

But it wasn't a game she would continue to play. Not with a guy like Mike, who wanted so much more than a one-night fling. And not when the kind of commitment he wanted would lead to love and marriage, which was more than Simone could—or would—give to anyone.

Too bad she hadn't been able to get Mike to believe that.

Yet, in part, she could understand why.

On the night they'd made love, she hadn't had any of her usual intimacy issues, so the sex had been incredible.

In fact, they'd made love until they'd run out of condoms, and she'd lost count of the climaxes she'd had.

But as the morning sun began to peer through the slats of the miniblinds, Simone had awakened, the sheets tangled at their feet and the scent of lovemaking in the air.

Dawn had brought forth a sobering reality, just as the gong sounding midnight had broken the spell cast on Cinderella.

Simone could no longer keep up the pretense in the light of day, so she'd slipped out of bed, grabbed a robe and found an excuse to send Mike on his way.

She just wished she could do the same thing with the memory of their romantic bedroom antics.

A sharp, whining cry tore through the house, and Simone threw off the covers and jumped out of bed.

Poor little Wags.

What in the world had Woofer done to him?

When she reached the kitchen, Wags had stopped his cries and sat next to Woofer at the gate, their tails swishing across the linoleum floor as though the whining had been a ploy to draw her back to them.

Nevertheless, she picked up Wags and looked him over carefully.

There wasn't any sign of blood.

"Darn you guys," she uttered.

If Mike had been home, she would have called and insisted he come pick up Wags. But he was on duty tonight.

And she was stuck until his shift ended.

* * *

At seven-fifteen the next morning, Simone finally climbed out of bed and, while exhausted, gave up any hope of getting a solid block of sleep. Thanks to the dogs, who'd whined and begged to be allowed to run free in the house all night, she'd slept fitfully. And since Wags wasn't housebroken, she'd had to make repeated trips outside.

The trouble was, she hadn't made it two feet out of her bedroom when she was laid low by a wave of nausea, followed by an annoying case of the dry heaves.

Being pregnant wasn't any fun at all, and she wanted to blame Mike, the stars or just plain bad luck, but the only one responsible was the pale, red-eyed, wild-haired woman staring back at her in the bathroom mirror.

After washing her face with cool water, she'd taken the dogs out to the backyard. Now she stood in the middle of the dew-drenched lawn in her pale green bathrobe and a pair of fuzzy pink slippers that had seen better days. She watched Woofer, who was—*hopefully*—teaching Wags what he should be doing outdoors and not inside on the kitchen floor.

The sky was overcast, and a wintry chill that had been absent yesterday urged her to slide her hands into the pockets of her robe.

She didn't want to be outside; she wanted to go back to bed.

God, what was she going to do?

She had to go to work this afternoon and had planned to leave Wags and Woofer in the yard alone, but they still needed supervision.

Mike wouldn't get off until six this evening, so she

was stuck without any chance of taking a nap before her shift started. That is, unless she found someone else to puppy-sit.

Think, she told herself. There had to be someone she could call.

Oh, wait.

Talk about lightbulb moments.

Maybe Millie would take Wags and keep him at Tails a Waggin' today. Then Simone could get some sleep before she had to work.

"Come on, you guys." She turned and headed up the back steps to the service porch, the dogs on her heels. She was going to call Mike at the station and tell him he could pick up Wags at the pet store when he got off work.

Once inside the house, she grabbed the phone book and looked for the number, then placed a call to the Walnut River Fire Department.

Woofer, who couldn't have gotten much sleep either, curled up at her feet, while Wags took off, exploring the part of the house that had been off limits to him all night.

Someone grabbed the phone on the second ring. "Fire department."

She didn't recognize the man who'd answered, but supposed it didn't matter. "This is Simone Garner. Is Mike O'Rourke available?"

"He sure is. I'll get him for you."

She was placed on hold for a moment or two, until a familiar voice came over the line.

"Hey, Simone. How's it going?" His tone was light and upbeat.

Hers, unfortunately, was *not*. "This isn't going to work, Mike."

"What's the matter?"

"The *dogs*. I didn't get any sleep last night. I'm going to have to ask Millie Baxter if she'll look after Wags so I can get some rest before I have to go to the hospital. And I hope she'll say yes. If so, can you pick him up at Tails a Waggin'?"

"Sure."

"You'll have to watch them tonight. Woofer isn't always happy about sharing his territory with a pesky pup, so sometimes they'll have to be separated." She glanced up long enough to see that Wags had returned, carrying something in his mouth.

When he growled as though he'd captured a pint-size prowler and was going to shake the life out of it, she took a closer look at what he'd locked his teeth onto.

Her shoe!

"Oh, no!" She dropped the phone on the counter and hurried toward Wags, who had chomped down on one of the brand-new black heels that she'd spent entirely too much money on.

But the moment Wags saw her coming, he dashed off, taking the shoe with him.

She'd probably never have reason to wear it again anyway, but that wasn't the point. "Come back here with that! You're going to ruin it."

As Wags ran through the house, dodging her at every turn, she swore under her breath.

Now this *was* something she could blame on Mike.

Mike gripped the receiver and strained to hear what was going on at Simone's house.

"Honey?" The endearment slipped out before he

could catch himself, and when there was no response from her, he blew out a sigh of relief.

What in the hell was going on over there?

He could hear her yelling at Wags, who'd undoubtedly taken something of value.

"No, Wags. No!" she said. "Bad dog."

He heard the approaching footsteps as she returned to the phone.

When she got back on the line, he asked, "What happened?"

"Wags chewed up my brand-new shoe."

Uh-oh. The puppy was going to wear out his welcome, if he hadn't done so already.

Maybe Mike had better find him a home with one of the guys in the department who had a family. He'd have to ask around.

"I'm really sorry about the shoe, Simone. I'll buy you another pair."

"You don't have to do that. I probably wouldn't have worn them again anyway. It's just that…that…" She sniffled, then broke into tears.

Damn. Simone *never* cried. At least, not out loud or in front of anyone. He'd seen emotion well in her eyes, but she'd always managed to hold it back. So what was with the tears?

Maybe it was that time of the month.

Of course, it could be something else. A buildup of some kind of stress, and Wags had been the last straw.

Either way, Mike had dumped the puppy on her, and the timing had been bad. Talk about guilt trips.

"I'm really sorry for the trouble I put you through, Simone."

"You'd *better* be sorry." She sniffled again, the words practically drowning in her throat. "See what happens when I don't get my rest? I fall apart."

"Aw, don't do that…"

As much as he dreaded the sound of her crying, a part of him liked to see the emotional side of her; it was so rare that anyone did.

Again she sniffled, and he wished he was there to put an arm around her, to let her lean on him.

"I can't handle this two nights in a row, Mike."

And he couldn't handle her tears—at least, not at a distance.

"I'll take care of everything," he said, not sure that he could. "If you drive to the pet store and ask Millie to look after Wags, I'll pick him up there when I get off duty. Then, if you don't mind, I'll sleep on your couch and take care of the dogs for you tonight. And when you get home from work, you can go into your bedroom, close the door and get a full night's sleep."

It was a last-ditch effort to pull things back together, and he really expected her to say no, to suggest he and Wags find somewhere else to hang their hats.

But she surprised him. "Okay. But if *that* doesn't work, you'll have to figure out something else."

Nice save. "Okay. Will do."

"I'll leave a key under the potted plant on my porch."

A grin tugged at his lips. He'd been hoping she would give him a key to her place, although he had to admit, these weren't quite the circumstances he'd had in mind.

But hey. He wouldn't complain.

A selfish side of him wanted to hold on to every little inch Simone gave him.

* * *

Later that afternoon, while seated at the desk at the nurses' station and reading the doctor's orders on one of the patient files, Simone yawned, wishing she could curl up in a corner and take another nap.

Bless Millie for keeping Wags earlier today.

Upon returning home from the pet store, Simone had slept for several hours, then showered and got ready for work.

So why was she still so tired?

The only explanation was pregnancy hormones, which meant she'd have to get used to feeling sluggish.

She glanced at the clock displayed on the wall that was directly across from the nurses' desk: 8:34.

It had been fairly quiet this evening, just the typical Wednesday-night complaints. They'd treated a toddler with a case of croup, a woman with a sliced finger that required sutures and a teenager whose intestinal flu had left him dehydrated.

Currently, they were examining a child with a broken thumb, as well as a middle-aged woman who'd fallen off a scooter and presented with a nasty scrape on her knee and a sprained wrist.

Just steps away, Dr. Ella Wilder was making notes in the injured woman's chart.

At twenty-nine, Ella was one of the youngest doctors on staff. She was also one of the most attractive.

Her hair, dark brown and straight, was cut in a neat bob that reminded Simone of the style worn by flappers in the Roaring Twenties. It suited her.

And so did her chosen profession.

Ella Wilder had come from a long line of doctors.

Her father, Dr. James Wilder, had been chief of staff before his recent death. Her oldest brother, Peter, an internist, was the acting chief of staff until a replacement could be found. Another brother, David, a renowned plastic surgeon who'd been living in Los Angeles, had just relocated here in Walnut River, where he would open a practice.

Only Anna, Ella's adopted older sister, had opted for a different career path.

From what Simone had gathered, the two sisters had been close growing up, but there was a strain between Anna and all of her siblings now.

Simone, an only child, didn't understand family dynamics, nor did she try to. Suffice it to say, she found it best to keep her nose to herself and just do her job.

Still, Simone liked Ella, a young woman who'd recently completed her residency in orthopedics at Boston Mass and now worked at Walnut River General. Simone wouldn't exactly say they were close, since she didn't warm to many people, but there was something about Ella that Simone admired.

"Dr. Wilder," Simone said to the orthopedist, "when you have a moment, Dr. Fitzgerald would like you to take a look at some X-rays. Jeffrey Colwell, the little red-haired boy in 4-A, broke his thumb and, apparently, knocked the growth plate out of whack."

"All right. I'm almost finished here."

Unable to help herself, Simone yawned again, and Ella chuckled.

Simone felt a little guilty. She prided herself on not missing work more than a handful of days in the last fifteen years, but maybe she should have called in sick today.

"I'm afraid I didn't get much sleep last night," she admitted.

Ella slid a glance her way and smiled. "I hope you had a good reason for staying awake—like a special man in your life. Maybe a handsome paramedic."

There was a glow to Ella these days, which was undoubtedly due to the "special man" in her own life, J. D. Sumner, who had recently resigned from his position with Northeastern HealthCare, the conglomerate hoping to take over Walnut River General.

But Ella was jumping to a conclusion Simone didn't want anyone to make.

"I hate to blow your theory to smithereens," Simone said, "but my *special someone* is a puppy."

"Oh, really?" Ella closed the file in which she'd been writing. "You adopted another dog, a playmate for Woofer?"

"No. I'm puppy-sitting for Mike O'Rourke."

Ella's grin broadened, and her eyes glimmered. "I was wondering how you two were doing. That guy is crazy about you."

The day after Peter's cocktail party, while talking privately to Ella, Simone had let it slip that she and Mike had slept together. After all, Ella had seen the two of them locked in a heated kiss beside Mike's Jeep the night before.

Simone couldn't blame Ella for wondering, but not everyone was destined for a romantic happy ending.

"Mike's a wonderful man," Simone admitted. "And he'll be a great catch for some lucky woman. But I'm a loner, and I always have been."

Hooking up with anyone, even a female roommate, would be tough on Simone, who'd grown comfortable with the peace and quiet at home. Of course, having an additional dog around was going to push her comfort level to the limit, but Mike was supposed to be looking for a place that would allow him to keep Wags. So, hopefully, her life would be back on track soon.

"You'll have to forgive me for wishing it had been the man keeping you awake instead of his dog."

Simone yawned again. "And you'll have to excuse me. Boy, what I wouldn't give to go home early and call it a night."

"Give me a moment to check that X-ray of Jeffrey's thumb," Ella said, "then you can join me for a cup of coffee in the doctors' lounge."

"All right." Simone doubted that the caffeine would be good for the baby, but she also needed to be able to function while at work. She wasn't going to get off until eleven. Maybe half a cup would be okay.

Fifteen minutes later, as Jeffrey and his mother prepared to head home with his hand stabilized in a cast, Ella returned. "Come on. Let's take a quick break before we get another rush."

After letting the E.R. resident and a fellow nurse know where she could be found, Simone joined Ella in the employee lounge, where they poured two cups of coffee and took a seat at the table.

"I've been off for a couple of days," Simone said. "So fill me in. What's the latest news about Northeastern HealthCare?"

The question shouldn't have surprised Ella. After all, it was on everyone's mind.

The threatened NHC takeover had many of the medical staff up in arms. The hospital had a reputation of providing the human touch and the kind of medical treatment patients deserved, while NHC was known in the industry for focusing on the bottom line at the expense of patient care.

"Well," Ella said, taking a sip of her coffee, "the attorney general's office has decided to investigate the claims of insurance fraud."

Simone had known that the state examiner's office claimed that the hospital was keeping patients longer than necessary and billing for treatment that wasn't given. She blew out a sigh. "I know we tend to keep patients longer than the average, but that's because we don't want to rush them out of the hospital too soon. I can't believe there's anything fraudulent going on here."

"I can't, either," Ella said. "But I don't like what a charge like that means in regard to an NHC takeover."

"Neither do I." Simone rested her cup on the table, yet held it in both hands. "If the hospital is found to be at fault, profits will go down and we'll have problems operating. Then NHC can swoop in like a superhero and save the hospital's reputation by including it in their 'family.'"

"Exactly." Ella glanced at her watch. "Where did the last hour go? I need to call it a day. I've been here since early this morning."

"You've got to be tired, too," Simone said. "Maybe you shouldn't have had the coffee."

"It's definitely been a long shift, which is the reason I wanted a bit of caffeine." Ella smiled, her eyes glimmering and her cheeks taking on a pretty flush. "J.D. has been staying with his dad since he quit NHC, but today we started living together, and we're having a celebratory dinner as soon as I get home."

The couple had been seeing a lot of each other for the past two months, and apparently things had gotten serious. Ella's happiness was impossible to ignore.

"Congratulations," Simone said. "Is he taking you out?"

"No, we're eating in. In fact, he's cooking and even has a bottle of champagne chilling. Apparently, I'm in for a romantic evening." She grinned. "So I need to get out of here."

Simone could understand why. "Have a wonderful night."

"Thanks. I intend to."

Simone's thoughts drifted to the man who was waiting at her house.

Of course, it wasn't the same.

Even if Mike thought that it should be.

Chapter Five

Mike, whose primary motivation for being at Simone's house *wasn't* because of the dogs, had gone grocery shopping when he'd gotten off work. And now that Simone was due home within minutes, he had a late-night snack ready for her.

He'd prepared a platter of cheese, crackers and fresh fruit for them to munch on, and if she was really hungry, he had all the fixings for a Dagwood-style sandwich.

Now all he had to do was wait.

Ever since he'd picked up Wags from the pet shop, where the puppy had been harassing Popeye Baxter all day rather than Woofer, the little guy had been playing hard. And now both dogs were resting near the hearth, where a steady flame licked the logs Mike had just added to the fire.

Simone's little house looked especially warm and

cozy tonight. The candles he'd lit and placed on the fireplace mantel gave it a romantic glow.

In truth, Mike hoped Simone liked the idea of coming home to a guy who loved her, a guy who knew what she needed without being asked.

As a car sounded outside, alerting him to her arrival, he met her at the door. Wags, apparently, was too tuckered out to even care that someone had entered, and Woofer merely raised his head and assured himself that Simone was home and that all was now well in his world.

"Good evening," Mike said as Simone hung up her jacket on a hook by the door.

Even after a tiring shift at work and wearing a pair of blue scrubs, she was an attractive woman who could turn his heart on end with a smile.

She scanned the small living room, took in the sight of the fresh flowers he'd placed on the coffee table. "What's that?"

"A peace offering," Mike said. "From Wags. He may not look very contrite at the moment, but he's very sorry for being such a pain in the butt last night."

A smile stretched across Simone's face, but he couldn't help noting the hint of crescent shadows under her eyes. He suspected they looked worse in the warm glow from the flickering candles.

He didn't mention how worn and tired she appeared, though. But he would do whatever he could to see that she got plenty of sleep tonight.

"If you're hungry, I have something for you to eat. And if not, I'll put it in the fridge."

"Thanks," she said. "That was sweet. A little snack

sounds good. If I don't keep something in my stomach, I get…"

"You get what?"

She gave a half shrug. "I get a little shaky. No big deal."

"You need to have that blood test. Did you call your doctor like you said you would?"

"Yes. And I have an appointment next week."

"Good."

Mike went into the kitchen and brought out a tray bearing the cheese, crackers and fruit platter, as well as a bottle of merlot, a corkscrew and two goblets. "I also thought a little wine before bed might help you unwind and fall asleep easier."

"I'd better pass on the wine, but there's some apple juice in the refrigerator. That sounds a lot better to me."

Was she afraid of the effect alcohol might have on her? That it might lower her inhibitions like last time they'd spent the evening together? That she might let down her guard and allow herself to feel again?

If so, he hoped she didn't think he was trying to ply her with wine. He'd only meant to set a romantic ambience, not get her into bed. The next time they made love, he wanted her to be completely sober and still willing. And, more important, he didn't want her to have any regrets in the morning.

"Look at this cheese plate." A smile that reached her soulful brown eyes sent his pulse topsy-turvy. "Have the guys down at the department been reading magazines on entertaining? This is pretty, as well as appetizing."

"Actually, a lady Leif has been dating invited a few of us over to watch the game and she set out a tray like this. It was pretty cool, and I thought you'd agree." He shrugged, cheeks warming. He hoped she didn't think he'd gone over the top.

"It's a nice touch," she said. "No one has ever prepared anything special for me."

Someone ought to.

And often.

"Then you're welcome."

As Mike turned to get the juice for her, she stopped him. "I'll get it. Why don't you have a seat and unwind. I took care of the dogs yesterday, so I know how tiring that can be."

"Actually," Mike said, glancing to the hearth where the canines lay side by side, "they weren't that bad tonight."

He'd taken them out in the backyard and thrown a ball to them until they were both worn-out and ready to settle down.

While Simone was in the kitchen, Mike poured a glass of wine for himself.

She'd just returned and settled into a comfortable position on the couch when her phone rang.

"Uh-oh." She furrowed her brow as she turned and reached for the telephone that rested on the lamp table. "I don't know who it could be at this hour."

"A woman called earlier," he said, "but she wouldn't leave her name. I told her you wouldn't get home until after eleven."

Mike watched as Simone snagged the receiver and answered on the second ring.

"Hello?" The furrow in her brow grew deeper. "Yes, it is."

He wasn't sure what was going on, but he listened to

her side of the conversation. It obviously wasn't a wrong number, but who the hell called people after eleven o'clock at night?

"That's too bad. No, I didn't know." She raked a hand through her hair, as though forgetting she wore it held back in a clip. Then she stood. "Would you please give me your number. I'd like to have it in case I need to speak to you later."

She made her way to the small rolltop desk against the wall and pulled out the top drawer. She fumbled inside until she withdrew a notepad and pen. Then she made a note.

"Thank you. I'll…uh…call her first thing in the morning."

Mike tensed, his senses on alert. Just from listening to Simone's side of the conversation, the news sounded serious.

She cleared her throat. "Yes, well…I don't know why she didn't call me, either."

When she hung up the phone, she remained standing, her back to him. She'd always carried herself with strength and pride, but her shoulders slumped and she blew out a heavy sigh.

Mike put down his glass and made his way toward her. "Is everything okay, honey?"

Damn, there went the endearment again. But this time, he wasn't sorry he'd let it slip out. Not when he sensed she needed some tenderness.

"I…uh…yeah. I'm fine." She turned to him, her eyes red and welling with tears. "It's just…well, my mom found a lump in her breast last week. But for some reason, she didn't want to bother me with the news.

That was a friend of hers who took it upon herself to call and let me know. She figured, even if my mom and I weren't close, that I was a nurse and could answer some of her questions and put her at ease."

Mike slid his arms around her, and she leaned into his embrace, resting her head against his chest.

He held her for a while, providing her with all he had to offer. His sympathy, his heart.

Finally, as she drew away, her gaze caught his, and he saw the pain inside. The grief.

What did one say to a woman who'd just learned of her mother's frightening discovery?

"That's just like my mom," Simone said, tears spilling from her eyes.

"What do you mean?"

She wiped the moisture from her cheeks and sniffed. "Needless to say, I'm concerned about her health and sorry she's struggling with all that lump could mean, but this is the kind of thing a mother should share with her daughter, whether she's a nurse or not. And it hurts to be reminded of just how lousy our relationship is. Especially if her condition proves to be life-threatening and I stand to lose her without ever having the kind of bond other mothers and daughters have."

Mike didn't know what to say, what to do. He couldn't get a handle on how a woman might feel upon finding a lump in her breast. Nor did he have any idea what that woman's daughter might be going through.

He figured they'd both be scared, anxious.

A simple, well-meant "I'm sorry" slid out. Yet it seemed so…inadequate.

"I'm sorry, too. And not just because of the news. I'm used to having my mom shut me out. She's been doing that to me for years. But I got the feeling that her friend thought I was too busy to be bothered. And that's simply not true."

"I know it isn't." If anyone had a heart for a person who was ill or hurting, it was Simone. And Mike was sorry that she and her mom were not close.

Maybe, in its own way, a diagnosis like this might draw the two of them together again. He hoped so; he couldn't imagine what his life would be like without the love and support of his family.

A shank of glossy hair had fallen from the clip Simone wore; now the strands hung along her cheek. Mike brushed them aside. "If you need anything, if your mom needs anything, you can count on me for help."

"Thanks."

"That's what friends…and lovers are for." As he brushed a kiss across her forehead, she gripped his waist as though hanging on to him, to everything his offer held.

When her lips parted, tempting him to place his mouth on hers, he was lost in a whirl of desire. He half expected her to push him away, but she slipped her arms around his neck and drew him closer instead.

It had been so long…

Too long.

The kiss deepened, and their tongues mated, sweeping and swirling in sleek, hot need. He couldn't get enough of her taste, of her touch, of her scent. And he held her tight, yearning to make them one.

Still, he wouldn't push. Wouldn't make the first move toward the bedroom. He'd been serious when he'd vowed that the next time they made love it would be at Simone's invitation, and she wouldn't need even a drop of alcohol to influence her decision.

As his hormones pumped, as his blood pounded in need, he reined in his desire to the point he thought he might die. And when she placed her hands on his chest and pushed him away, he thought he surely would.

"I'm sorry, Mike. But I can't. I just can't do this."

Oh, she *could*. And she *had*. But he knew better than to argue.

She unclipped the barrette in her hair, then combed her fingers through the strands. "I'm not the kind of woman who wants or needs a man in my life."

"You may not *want* one. But you definitely *need* one." And Mike was the man she needed most.

His suspicion that she'd been hurt in the past only deepened now.

She strode back to the coffee table and picked at a clump of grapes he'd placed next to the slices of cheese. "In the three or so years you've known me, how many times have you seen me with a man—romantically speaking? How many times have I actually gone out on a date?"

"That's not healthy," he said.

"I'm not very good at relationships, so it's easier this way."

He couldn't buy that. Still, it had been five or six weeks since the two of them had slept together. But he had no idea how long it had been for her prior to that.

Too long, he suspected. The last guy she'd been involved with must have done a real number on her self-esteem.

"Can't you be content to let us just be friends?"

God only knew how long he could keep this up. His hope was that she'd give in to her true feelings before he grew tired of waiting.

Damn. He was only human.

"I'll take whatever you can give me," he said.

At least that was his plan for now.

The next morning, Simone woke to the sounds of dogs barking. She rolled over in bed, raised up on an elbow and peered through the curtains. In the backyard, Mike was playing ball with Wags and Woofer, who obviously hadn't learned the rules of Fetch.

But she had to give Mike credit for trying to teach them how to bring the little rubber ball back to him and not keep it as a well-earned prize.

What was she going to do about that man?

If she believed in the power of true love, if she believed that she could become involved in any kind of lasting relationship, she would definitely consider making Mike a part of her life.

But she knew her own flaws, as well as her strengths.

When Cynthia Pryor, her mom's neighbor, had called last night to inform Simone of something another mother would have disclosed on her own, she'd been completely taken aback. Not just by the terrible news, but by the blatant reminder that she and her mom had never been close, that they never would be.

And thanks to their dysfunctional relationship, Simone would never be able to create a warm, loving family of her own.

After the call, when Mike had held her, when he'd

kissed her, she'd wanted so badly to accept all that he'd been willing to give her.

But how could she when she knew she'd always hold back? When she knew she'd always retreat to that special place in her mind where no one could ever hurt her again?

As she climbed from bed, another bout of morning sickness struck with a vengeance, and she hurried to the bathroom. When it was all over—God, she hated being sick—she washed her face, returned to the bedroom and sat on the edge of mattress. Then she dialed her mother's house.

After the third ring, a click sounded. Simone opened her mouth to respond, but when the canned voice of her mom's answering machine began its recitation, she blew out a ragged sigh instead.

"You have reached 518–555–2467. I can't come to the phone right now, but if you leave your name and number, I'll return your call at my earliest convenience."

Simone cleared her throat. "Hi, Mom. It's me. I just wanted to touch base and see how you've been. Please give me a call when you can. It's—" she glanced at the clock on the bureau "—it's ten-fifteen on Thursday. I have to go into work this afternoon around three, but I should be close to home until then. I love you."

As she hung up the phone, she realized that she always ended her calls that way. *I love you.*

But did she?

Did that little girl inside of her still exist? The one who'd desperately wanted to hear those three little words repeated and know, without a doubt, that her mother truly meant them?

No. That lonely child had faded into the past when

Simone hit high school, where she learned that she could get the affirmation, respect and attention she craved from her teachers. So, as a result, she studied hard and excelled—especially in science.

At one time, she'd actually thought about going to medical school, but the cost was prohibitive, especially without any family support. So she'd settled for nursing school, where she graduated at the top of her class.

Fifteen years ago, she landed a job at Walnut River General and worked on any floor she was assigned. But she soon found her real calling in the emergency room, where she gained the respect of patients, coworkers and administrators alike.

One nice thing about the E.R. was that Simone could become personally involved with the patients for a few hours, then was able to back off as they either went home or were sent to other floors in the hospital.

Yes, she'd overcome a lot in the past thirty-seven years, but she still found it difficult to actually connect with people.

When the rubber ball Mike and the dogs had been playing with hit the side of the house, the wooden window frame and the glass shook and shuddered.

Simone peered out into the yard to see what was going on outside.

Through the pane of glass separating them, Mike caught her gaze, smiled and shrugged at the same time. Then he mouthed, "I'm sorry."

She was sorry, too. Sorry that she couldn't pin her heart and her dreams on Mike O'Rourke. That she couldn't create something she'd never had.

Once upon a time, she'd hoped and prayed to have

what other children had been blessed with, but that dream had faded along with that little brown-haired girl who used to cry herself to sleep each night.

The child whose mother had looked at her newborn for the very first time and determined that she was unlovable.

Mike had found his true calling when he'd pursued EMT training at the local junior college.

In fact, he loved everything about his job—the adrenaline rush, the satisfaction of saving a life.

Sure, there were times when it was tough, times when he came upon an accident victim too late to be of any help.

He didn't like having to look into the eyes of a victim's family and tell them there was nothing left to do but to call the coroner. But he accepted that as part of life, as part of his job.

Tonight, just after eight o'clock, he and Leif were sitting around the television at the station with several other guys when the next call came in, and the men all sprung into action.

Four and a half minutes later, they arrived at the scene of a car accident that had occurred when a seventy-six-year-old woman ran a stop sign at the intersection of Lexington and Pine, broadsiding a vehicle driven by a sixteen-year-old boy.

The teenager in a white Honda Accord had suffered a possible skull fracture, lacerations to the face and a broken collarbone.

The elderly woman had been hurt, too. But Mike suspected she might have had a seizure or ministroke while behind the wheel, which had probably caused the accident. They wouldn't know for sure until she was examined at the hospital.

Eight minutes after the arrival of the paramedics on the scene, both victims were loaded in the ambulance and en route to Walnut River General.

As Leif and Mike monitored the vitals of the victims, the flashing red lights and siren alerted the other cars on the road to pull over and let the emergency vehicle pass.

Simone was working tonight, and Mike hoped that after the patients were stabilized he'd have a chance to see her, to talk to her.

After passing both the teenager and the woman to the E.R. staff, Mike and Leif stopped by the nurses' desk to complete the necessary paperwork.

"Hey," Leif said, nodding toward an open doorway, where Simone stood at the bedside of a young girl who had a gash in her leg. "If you're both working, who's looking after the dogs?"

"We decided to leave them alone tonight and hope for the best." Mike glanced up from the form he'd signed. "I sure hope they don't disturb her neighbors. They get a little loud and rambunctious sometimes."

The radio squawked, and Leif responded, alerting dispatch that the medics were available again. When he'd done so, he excused himself. "I'm going to get a soda. Want me to get you one?"

"No, I'm fine."

As Leif walked away, Mike took the time to study Simone, to watch her interact with a frightened little girl he guessed to be about six or seven years old.

Simone took a disposable glove from a box, blew into the opening to create a balloon, then knotted the end.

The fingers stood straight up, resembling either a rooster's comb or a kid's Mohawk. Then she took a black pen and drew a pair of eyes above the thumb and a mouth below it.

The result brought forth a smile on the child's face, providing some relief from her pain and fear.

Why couldn't Simone see in herself what he saw in her—the compassion, the dedication, the heart of a woman who truly cared?

A woman who would make a great wife and mother.

In the past, Mike had sowed his share of wild oats. But as family holidays came and went, each one growing bigger with another new in-law or the birth of a baby, he'd begun to feel a growing urge to find a mate, settle down and create a home and family of his own.

Simone was a challenge, though.

As she returned to the desk where Mike continued to stand, she tossed a pretty smile his way. "Wags and Woofer must be doing okay. Otherwise, I suspect Mrs. McAllister, the woman who lives next door to me, would have called to complain by now."

"I knew they'd eventually learn how to get along." He'd taken that same stance with Simone, hoping that she'd get used to having him around, that she'd let down her guard and quit fighting her feelings for him.

"Did you ever get ahold of your mother?" he asked. "How's she doing?"

Simone's movements slowed to a snail's pace. "I'm afraid I really don't know. We've been playing phone tag."

"I'm sorry to hear that."

Simone gave a half shrug. "Actually, that's par for the course."

"Because you're both so busy?" Mike had a brother who worked odd hours and was hard to find at home.

"My mom and I never seem to connect." She crossed her arms and shifted her weight to one hip.

"Maybe you ought to try and talk to her again this evening," he suggested, "when you get a break."

"We'll see."

"I guess you'll want to call her when you can have some privacy."

Simone scanned the E.R.

Looking to see who was listening? he wondered.

She uncrossed her arms and straightened, distancing herself from the conversation. "I'm probably the last one on earth she really wants to hear from. So I'm going to let her call me if and when she's ready."

Mike watched as Simone returned to her young patient, the rubber soles of her shoes squeaking upon the tile. He'd suspected that the person who'd hurt her had been a man. That the wrongs she'd suffered and her subsequent pain might be something he could heal and rectify.

But maybe he'd been wrong.

Chapter Six

Three days later, Mike was still coming by the house to watch the dogs whenever he could, and Simone continued to drop off Wags at the Baxters' store when she didn't want to leave the dogs alone.

"I feel like a real parent," he'd told her earlier as he prepared to leave for his next shift at the station.

She'd imagined him as a father, too—to *real* children; not the kind with four paws and fur.

"This isn't the same," she'd responded, wanting to change the subject to one that wasn't so…so steeped in truth.

Something warm and tender had simmered in his gaze, something that threatened to not only pull her in, but to drag her through a rush of emotion.

"I can't help wondering what our kids would look like," he'd said, "if you and I were to have them."

The statement had nearly knocked her to the floor, and she'd struggled to recover.

Ever since learning that she was pregnant, she'd been thinking a lot about the baby they'd created and had tried to imagine whether it was a girl or a boy. But she couldn't allow herself to focus on the child being theirs—or even his. Instead, she'd forced herself to think about the joy the baby would bring to its new parents, a couple who'd been hoping and praying for a child to love.

A couple like Fred and Millie.

"You'll make a fabulous father," she'd told him. "But I'm not the maternal type. Trust me on that, okay?"

He'd cupped her face with both hands. "And I say that you *are*."

For a long, heart-stopping moment, she'd wanted to believe him—for his sake.

And for the child's.

But she knew things Mike didn't. Things that would make him change his mind.

"You're going to be late," she'd told him, trying to shoo him out the door before she was forced to tell him the truth sooner than she was ready to do so.

Now she'd just parked in front of Tails a Waggin'.

"Here we are," she told Wags as she reached for the handle of his carrier and took him inside the pet shop.

Simone had called the store earlier, and Millie had agreed to take Wags home for the night. Although Simone was feeling better about leaving the dogs alone, she didn't like the idea of Wags being unsupervised inside the house. Not when he chewed everything in sight and still wasn't housebroken.

She could, of course, leave the dogs outside, but there

was a biting chill in the air, and dark clouds had gathered on the horizon. Because of the threatening weather, they couldn't stay in the yard tonight. But if Wags stayed with Millie, Woofer could be left in the house alone.

"Look who's here," Millie said to Popeye Baxter, who wore a yellow bandanna around his neck and sat next to the register. "Your little friend is back."

Simone watched as Popeye perked up in response to the news, and a smile crept across her face. Woofer was still getting used to having Wags around, so it was nice to think that Popeye found him entertaining.

"I sure appreciate you taking Wags for me," Simone said. "And hopefully, I won't need to impose on you too many more times. Mike is hoping to find a place, and his real estate agent called about a house that sounds promising. She's going to show it to him on his next day off."

"Fred and I don't mind watching Wags." Millie took the dog carrier from Simone and set it on the counter. Then she unhooked the latch, swung open the little door and reached inside. "Are the dogs getting along any better yet?"

"With each other? Yes. But when I got in last night, there was a note left on my door by the woman who lives next door. Apparently, they were barking and making an awful racket while I was gone."

"That's too bad," Millie said. "You don't want to upset your neighbors."

Simone didn't like to be kept awake by someone else's noise, either. She also tried to be considerate of the people who lived near her.

"Life is so much nicer when everyone in the neighborhood is on friendly terms," Millie added, giving

Wags a cuddle before setting him down on the floor so he could play.

It's not that Simone really cared about maintaining any kind of relationship with those who lived near her. She waved to a couple of people when she saw them in their yards or on the street, but for the most part, she kept to herself.

When at home, she preferred her privacy and wasn't interested in community gossip. Neither did she want just anyone to pop in unexpectedly for a leisurely cup of coffee and a chat.

Fortunately, her neighbors seemed to have read into her let's-not-get-too-chummy expressions and gave her plenty of space.

She couldn't say the same for Mike, though. He hadn't seemed to read anything into her words or her demeanor. She supposed it was flattering that he'd stuck it out so far, but he had more faith in her than she had in herself.

If she were to let his charm go to her head and allow something to develop between them, she would be crushed when it ended, just as she had been when Tom Nichols said he couldn't deal with a cold and unfeeling lover.

And if Mike made the same claim, it would be devastating since she cared more for Mike than she had for Tom.

A *lot* more.

Mike was a better man all the way around. And he was proving to be a good friend, too.

So why exchange their friendship for a temporary affair? It didn't make sense, especially when she had very few friends in her life.

"I'm really going to miss Wags when you quit bringing him by," Millie said. "He's such a sweetheart."

"He has his naughty moments, too. You ought to see the shoe he destroyed, the puddles he made on the hardwood floor and the fringe on the throw rug he chewed."

"Aw, you can't get mad at Wags for that," Millie said. "He's still a baby."

"I know. I try to keep that in mind." Simone tucked a strand of hair behind her ear. "By the way, speaking of babies, how's the adoption search coming along? Are you having any luck?"

"I'm afraid not." Millie scanned the store, as though searching for someone who might be eavesdropping.

Fred maybe?

Another customer?

"We were turned down again. And a couple of weeks ago, after another…" She blew out a sigh. "Well, let's call it another monthly disappointment. Anyway, Fred, bless his heart, took me for a long drive. We ended up at Crescent Lake, where we found a nice little spot and had a picnic—just the two of us. Then we prayed together, telling God how badly we wanted a child, but agreeing to abide by his will. If he wants us to have a baby, he'll provide one for us. And if not?" Millie smiled warmly. "Fred and I have complete peace about whatever happens."

Que sera, sera, Simone thought. What will be, will be.

"It won't be the end of the world if we don't have children," Millie said. "After all, there aren't too many couples who have what Fred and I've been blessed with. We have a loving, marital bond. We're business partners, too, and the very best of friends. A child would merely be frosting on a cake that is moist and rich in and of itself."

Simone wasn't a religious person. After all, she'd prayed countless times that her mother would love her when she'd been a little girl. And it just hadn't happened.

Who knew why some kids were conceived in love and others weren't. Why some were born into loving arms and others into a cold environment.

Or why some women could accept the love offered them when others were afraid to.

Either way, a relationship like the one Fred and Millie shared was rare in this day and age. The Baxters were fortunate.

And if they had a baby, it would be lucky, too.

Yet Simone admired their resolve to give up their dream of having a child of their own and to trust that things would work out—one way or another.

Still, she couldn't help thinking that her baby might be destined to be the frosting on the Baxter's cake.

Late that afternoon, while raindrops danced upon the hospital windows, Simone sat across from Isobel Suarez in the hospital cafeteria, where they'd each set down a tray carrying a cup of soup and a half sandwich.

Isobel, an attractive woman in her mid-thirties, with curly auburn hair and a ready smile, always had a kind word or a bit of wisdom to share. But then again, that shouldn't be a surprise. Isobel was also the hospital social worker, a job she'd had for the past ten years.

From the first day they'd met, Simone had found Isobel different from the others and easy to talk to. So gradually, she'd begun to open up to someone for the first time in her life.

Simone had eventually admitted why she and her

mother had never been close, a shameful secret Simone had stumbled upon by accident but had never discussed with anyone else.

At first, Simone had feared that Isobel might try to psychoanalyze her, but that hadn't been the case. Isobel knew how to be a true friend without letting her training and her degree get in the way.

"Can I share something with you?" Simone asked.

"Sure."

"In *confidence*," Simone added.

"Of course." Isobel laid down her spoon and pushed her cup of soup aside. "This sounds serious."

"It is." For a moment, Simone sat on her secret, clung to it, but she felt safe with Isobel. Still, the words came out softly, tentatively. "I'm…pregnant."

Isobel picked up her napkin and blotted her lips. "How do you feel about that?"

"Flabbergasted. Overwhelmed. Foolish. Afraid. Awestruck." Simone shrugged. "I think that about covers it."

Isobel placed her elbows on the table and leaned forward slightly. "What are you going to do?"

"Give the baby up for adoption."

"And the father will be okay with that?"

Simone's thoughts drifted to Mike, to the young paramedic who seemed to think she'd make a good wife and mother. The guy who had a slew of nieces and nephews and would love to have a kid of his own someday.

"I haven't told him about it yet," she admitted, "but when I do, I hope he'll eventually be able to see the wisdom in my decision."

Actually, she was afraid Mike would react positively

to the news. And that he'd try to talk her into marrying him and keeping the baby.

But what would he say when she was forced to level with him about the past, about her shortcomings?

The emotional scars that she carried would cause him to resent her someday.

Hadn't Simone come to resent her mother for the same reason?

She'd tried to tell Mike that he was barking up the wrong tree when it came to a long-term commitment. But he seemed to think that, with time, everything would work out between them.

Simone knew better, though. And she suspected that, as a social worker, her friend would agree with her.

"Is there any chance that you and the father might want to raise this child together?" Isobel asked.

"No. In spite of an age difference, our family backgrounds are completely opposite. So nothing lasting could ever come of a relationship with him."

Besides, Mike wanted so much more than Simone could give him.

"Sometimes opposites not only attract, but bring out the best in each other," Isobel said.

Simone reached across the table and placed her hand over her friend's. "I've told you about some of the pain I went through as a child, but I held back on the worst of it."

"You're a strong, dependable and resilient woman, Simone. It seems to me that you've overcome the emotional obstacles you faced."

Some of them, she supposed. "But I never learned the emotional skills needed to parent. Not by example, anyway. And for that reason, I'm afraid I'll fail the baby just as badly as my mother failed me."

Isobel's gaze snagged Simone's, soothing her in a pool of compassion and understanding.

Over the years, Simone may have shared certain details about past events with Isobel, but she'd never revealed the depth of her feelings, her fears.

"Adoption is best for everyone involved." The words came out sure, steady. Yet for a moment, something waffled inside. Something she couldn't quite put her finger on.

"You've got time to let your options simmer for a while," Isobel said. "And, after you do, I'm sure you'll make the right decision—whatever that might be."

"Thanks." Simone withdrew her hand and leaned back in her seat.

"There's something else you should keep in mind," Isobel added. "Just because you had a bad role model doesn't mean you're going to make the same mistakes. I happen to believe you'd make a wonderful mother someday—to this baby or to another."

Unfortunately, Simone didn't share the same faith or the same vision that Mike and Isobel had.

"Thanks for the vote of confidence, but I can't even begin to think of myself as a mom. Not with the mothering I had." Simone chuffed. "And even now, our mother/daughter relationship is limited to Christmas cards and an occasional phone call."

Isobel didn't comment. Other than sympathize, what could she say?

Of course, maybe she was thinking about how close she'd been to her own mother and how tough it had been to lose her. From what Simone had gathered, Isobel had moved in with her dad after her mom passed away. The two were very close.

Simone could hardly imagine a relationship like that. She reached for the cellophane-wrapped packet of crackers that had come with her soup. "My mom recently found a lump in her breast, and even though I've tried to contact her several times and left messages, she won't return my calls. She's completely shut me out."

"Fear of breast cancer can blindside a woman." Isobel took a sip of water. "I'm not trying to make excuses for the mistakes your mom made when you were growing up, but she may find it difficult to talk to anyone right now. You might need to be patient with her."

"You've got a point."

They returned to their meal, but Simone focused on the saltines she'd unwrapped. Looking right through the little squares as she pondered the only real option she had.

"How do you feel about open adoptions?" she asked Isobel. "Do they work? Would it be difficult watching a child grow up in someone else's home if everyone knows each other?"

"It depends upon the people involved. In my experience, open adoptions work out beautifully if the biological and the adoptive parents are able to put the child's best interests ahead of their own."

"I've got a couple in mind," Simone said. "But you're right. There's time for me to think things through. And if I should decide not to give the baby to someone I know, I'd like you to recommend a good agency that will help me find just the right parents."

"No problem. Tomorrow, when I have a chance, I'll

give you the names of several organizations I've worked with in the past."

Simone ought to feel relieved, yet handing over her child to strangers made her uneasy, too.

But how could she even consider dumping all her personal baggage on a poor defenseless baby?

Besides, even with the few friendships she had—Isobel and, more recently, Ella—she always held back—just as she feared she would do with a baby.

On top of that, children needed a primary caregiver, someone they could trust to see to all their needs, physical as well as emotional. They needed someone to kiss their owies and to make them cookies. Someone to tuck them in at night.

How could Simone give up her job to be a stay-at-home mom?

She loved everything about being an E.R. nurse—the pressure of being in a life-or-death situation, the competent and dedicated medical staff with whom she worked, the patients who rushed in with complaints and symptoms that were sometimes hard to diagnose.

Why, she even loved the hours she kept, never complaining about a night shift or two.

No, her life wasn't conducive to motherhood.

And she was a fool on those rare occasions when she allowed herself to think otherwise.

Nearly a week later, after Ella Wilder had treated a teenage boy who fell off a skateboard and broke his arm, Simone took the orthopedic surgeon aside. "There's a cake in the solarium to celebrate Dr. Randall's being hired as the new chief of staff."

Owen Randall was a cardiac surgeon who'd suffered a serious hand injury and could no longer perform the operations for which he was trained. But that didn't mean he wouldn't make a top-notch chief of staff.

Although he'd been hired from the outside and not from within, those who'd already met the man had talked about being impressed with his professionalism, as well as his people skills.

"Peter's very happy to be back in private practice," Ella said.

"I'm sure he is." With a new lady in his life—Bethany Holloway, a hospital board member—and a wedding on the horizon, Peter was undoubtedly glad to pass the baton to someone else and get back to his patients.

"Dr. Randall is in the solarium, as we speak," Simone said. "He's making himself accessible to the entire staff. He's also serving cake, which is chocolate, by the way."

Ella smiled. "My favorite. All right, let's stop by and congratulate our new boss."

The solarium was located on the first floor and looked out onto the hospital gardens, which had just begun to bloom with various displays of red, yellow and pink buds.

In the center of the room, Owen Randall, a stocky, fifty-something man with thinning silver hair, met Ella and Simone with a smile. He introduced himself, then handed them each a slice of cake. As he did so, the tip of his bright yellow-and-green tie dragged across the white, butter-cream frosting.

"Oops. Would you look at that?" His jovial chuckle reverberated in the lounge. "Another tie bites the dust."

The ability to laugh at himself was a good sign, Simone decided. It would make working under him much easier.

They made small talk with Dr. Randall, who seemed to be a friendly sort.

Simone wondered if he'd do as well in the chief-of-staff position as the late Dr. James Wilder had. She hoped so. James had been a well-liked and respected physician who'd put quality patient care above all else.

Since Ella and Simone were both on duty, they excused themselves, then carried their cake back to the nurses' station.

"There sure are a lot of changes going on around here," Ella said as she took a seat behind the desk.

"I know. I wonder if we'll have cake again on Saturday, when Henry Weisfield officially steps down as the hospital administrator."

"It's possible." Ella dug her fork into her slice of the chocolaty concoction and took a bite, obviously relishing the sweet taste. "You know, J.D. applied for Henry's job and…" She leaned in closer to Simone and lowered her voice. "From what we understand, he's being seriously considered for the position."

"I'd heard that," Simone said. "With J.D.'s business skills, I'm sure his chances of landing the administrator's job are excellent."

"I've certainly got my fingers crossed," Ella said.

"I'll bet they are." Simone glanced at Ella, only to see she had indeed crossed the fingers on both hands, one of which—her left—sported a sparkling diamond ring.

"Well, I'll be darned. You're engaged."

Ella beamed. "As of last night."

"Congratulations."

"Thanks." Ella took another bite of cake, seeming to enjoy every morsel.

Under usual circumstances, Simone would be doing the same. But the sugary taste wasn't sitting too well, and she didn't want to push herself or her sensitive stomach by eating any more than she already had.

"How goes the puppy-sitting?" Ella asked.

"So far, so good. Mike helps out a lot. But I'll be glad when he finds a place of his own soon."

"That's too bad. I was hoping that the two of you would hook up."

"Mike is, too." And while Simone had begun to think his feelings for her might be genuine, she just couldn't trust herself to be the kind of wife he expected and deserved.

"It doesn't surprise me that Mike is wishing for more. The guy's definitely in love." Ella scooped a dab of frosting from the top of her cake and popped it into her mouth. "And you're not going to be able to convince me that lust has anything to do with the way that man looks at you."

Okay, so Simone had to admit that she'd seen the way Mike looked at her, too. And that it didn't appear that he was only interested in sex.

But how long would his affection and loving glances last?

When would he look beyond her facade and see her for what she really was?

For a moment, Simone was tempted to tell Ella about the pregnancy, about her decision to give the baby up for adoption. After all, assuming she was able to carry the baby to term, it would be public knowledge soon enough.

She bit her tongue instead.

One emotional revelation like that was a record for Simone.

But two disclosures in less than a week?

No way.

The next person she told about her pregnancy would be the baby's father, but she just couldn't bring herself to tell him yet.

Simone may have reached a decision she could live with, but she didn't have a clue how to drop the bomb on Mike.

Chapter Seven

Late Thursday morning, after Mike met with Leif's sister and looked at a three-story Victorian-style home on Maple, he stopped by the New England Ranch Market. The trendy grocery store, a favorite of the locals, offered farm-fresh eggs, organic vegetables and an old-fashioned butcher shop that cut meat to order.

While pushing his cart through the aisles, he picked up a couple of chicken breasts, some red potatoes, fixings for a salad and the special ingredients needed for his killer vinaigrette dressing. Then, before heading to the checkout line, he stopped by the bakery section and picked up a lemon meringue pie—his favorite.

The guys in the department took turns with kitchen duty, and Mike, who'd had no experience cooking at all when he'd first been hired, had to ask his mom to teach him how to prepare some of his favorite family meals.

He'd even picked up a few culinary tricks from some of his coworkers and, while not what you'd call a pro, he knew how to fix a decent spread.

Now, as he climbed from his Jeep Wrangler, Woofer barked at the fence. Mike had a feeling it was more of a "Welcome back" than a "Don't even think about trespassing" announcement. Either way, little Wags followed suit.

It was kind of cool that the puppy had the watchdog lessons down pat. Too bad he wasn't doing as well when it came to getting housebroken.

Once on Simone's front porch, Mike shuffled the two grocery bags he held in his arms so he could ring the bell. He hoped Simone was okay with what he planned to do.

He had a key, so he could let himself in, but Simone wasn't working today, and he didn't want to overstep his boundaries.

She answered the door in her robe. Her hair was wrapped in a white towel turban, her scent powdery fresh with a hint of shampoo, soap and a citrusy body lotion that he'd grown accustomed to.

Damn, she sure smelled good.

But it had to be nearly noon. The times he'd spent the night on her sofa, she'd always showered first thing.

"Did you just wake up?" he asked.

"I wasn't feeling…" She cleared her throat. "Well, I woke up tired, so since I'm off today, I decided to go back to bed."

"Are you okay?" he asked, remembering that she was supposed to be going to the doctor. When was her appointment? What would the blood work show?

"I'm fine." She offered him a smile. "It's amazing what a little nap will do."

"Can I come in?"

"Oh. Sorry." She stepped aside so he could enter, then nodded at the bags he held in his arms. "What's that?"

"It's our dinner. I'm going to cook for you."

"You really don't have to." She tightened the sash of her robe—one that had faded from use and bore a light scent of detergent, giving it the fragrance of home and hearth. "I'll just fix myself a sandwich."

"Not tonight. We've got something to celebrate."

Her brow furrowed. "What are we celebrating?"

A sense of pride settled in his chest, a tinge of excitement. "I just made an offer on a house."

"No kidding?" She followed him into the kitchen. "Where's it located?"

"In Riverdale. Leif's sister knew I was looking for something that needed a little work, and as soon as she snagged the listing, she gave me a call. I met her first thing this morning, and she was right. It's just what I was looking for. So she wrote up my offer."

"That was certainly fast," Simone said. "It took me weeks to decide upon this place. I had to hire someone to come out and inspect it for me so that I could make sure it didn't have any unexpected problems."

Mike placed the bags on the countertop and began to remove the items he'd purchased. "I called my brother Aaron, and he stopped by to give me his opinion. But he agreed, the house needs a lot of work, but it's nothing major."

"Congratulations. I guess that *is* something to celebrate."

"Thanks. It's possible they won't accept my offer, but Karen feels pretty confident they'll be willing to negotiate." He removed the chicken breasts that had been wrapped in butcher paper and placed the package in her fridge, next to a gallon of milk.

That big plastic jug seemed like a pretty large amount for a single woman to purchase for herself. Maybe she was getting used to having Mike around.

He sure hoped so.

"Tell me about the house," she said.

"It's the old Dennison place. I'm not sure if you remember, but three or four weeks ago, Ethel Dennison fell and broke her hip. Leif and I got the call and transported her to the E.R. I think you were on duty that night, but you were working with someone else at the time."

Simone remembered the elderly woman who'd come in that night. "Ethel is a nice lady. I felt badly that she'd gotten hurt and that she would probably have to go into a convalescent home while she recuperated."

"Her only child, a daughter, lives in Ohio and insisted that it was time Ethel moved in with her."

"It's too bad she had to give up her home, but it's nice that she gets to be with her family."

"Yes, it is," he said. "Being with loved ones beats the heck out of going into a long-term-care facility."

Yes, it did. But just thinking about Mrs. Dennison and her plight brought a question to mind.

If something happened to Simone's mother, would she invite the woman to move in with her?

Sheesh. How far did one's obligation go to a biological relative who acted more like a stranger?

Did it go beyond those occasional phone calls and Christmas dinners eaten in silence?

The only thing that made her feel slightly better about envisioning the scenario was the fact that even if Simone were to make an offer like that, her mom probably wouldn't want to live with her.

"If they accept my price, Karen is going to ask them if I can rent the house from them until the close of escrow. And if they agree, Wags and I will be out of your hair in no time at all." Mike tossed her a boyish grin. "So you see? Now you have good reason to celebrate, too."

How could she say no to that?

Yet, for some reason, she didn't feel particularly relieved about having her home to herself again.

"So," Mike said, "now that I'm here, I'll take the dogs for a walk. I thought maybe Woofer would show Wags how it's done."

"That would be nice."

"You can walk with us, if you like. Or if you have any errands to run, go ahead. I'll take them by myself."

Actually, Simone had an appointment for a pedicure later this afternoon. And she wanted to pick up a new pair of nursing shoes, too. She also needed to replace her iron. Yesterday, before work, she'd been pressing a pair of scrubs when Wags got his head stuck behind the lamp table. She'd rushed to help him, tripped over the cord and knocked the iron onto the floor, breaking off the little spout that provided steam.

"Are you sure you don't mind going alone?" she asked.

"Not at all. Take the day off, go shopping, have lunch with a friend. Whatever."

His grin caused her heart to flip-flop, and for the

briefest moment, she had the urge to tell him no, that
she'd rather stick close to home and hang out with him
and the dogs.

But how lame was that?

Taking a walk and spending the day with Mike
might be counterproductive to everything she'd been
trying to tell him.

That he couldn't expect anything other than friendship from her.

It was late in the afternoon when Simone returned
from her errands, but she didn't find Mike or the dogs
inside the house.

She did see signs in the kitchen that he'd started
dinner. A covered pot sat on the stove, and a bottle of
red wine rested on the counter, uncorked and breathing.

She heard a noise outside, made her way to the back
door and glanced out the small window. She spotted him
standing on the patio and firing up the grill, the dog and
the puppy sitting on their haunches beside him.

Rather than let him know she was home, she stood
there a moment, enjoying the sight of man and beast
and nature.

Or rather, just the man.

Mike's efforts at the barbecue had caused a hank of
raven-black hair to fall across his brow. The intensity in
his expression as he stoked the fire was enough to cap-
tivate her, to make her think of a Scottish laird on a
windswept moor.

If Simone believed in miracles, if she believed that
he might be right about…

But she couldn't. Her mother had slowly whittled

away at her self-esteem and her ability to trust anyone with her true emotions.

Instead, she tore her attention away from Mike, fearing that, if he caught her eye, the attraction she just couldn't seem to kick would be too obvious. And if that happened, she could end up encouraging him to think the two of them could live happily ever after, rather than convince him they wouldn't.

After putting away the items she'd purchased while shopping—a pair of scrubs to go along with the nursing shoes, as well as an iron and a few other household cleaning products—she went into the kitchen and announced, "Hey, I'm back."

For a moment, her words had a honey-I'm-home ring to them, and she almost forgot that, when it came to love, she was a nonbeliever. At least, when it came to her and that particular emotion, she was.

Maybe she'd be better off coming clean with Mike about her past. About her irreparable scars. Then, when she finally leveled with him about the baby, he'd be more inclined to understand why she felt the way she did.

The door swung open, and Mike strode inside, as charming and hunky as ever. "Hey, beautiful. How was your day?"

Darn him. She almost felt pretty when she was with him. Even in a pair of jeans and a plain white cotton blouse.

She conjured a smile and lifted her right foot, which was wearing bright pink nail polish and a turquoise flip-flop. "It was great. I had a pedicure. See?"

His mouth quirked in a boyish grin that nearly buckled her knees. "Your toes look great. So does the rest of you."

Oh, yeah. She'd gotten a haircut while she was at the salon. She supposed she couldn't blame him for noticing. She usually wore it pulled back, out of her face.

"I like it down and curled under like that."

Yeah. Well… "Thanks." She combed her fingers through the strands, feeling them sluice along her hands, and struggled to find something else to say to that.

A change of topic would be good about now.

"What's for dinner?" she asked.

"Barbecued chicken, seasoned red potatoes and a salad that'll have you begging for the secret recipe of my vinaigrette dressing. But I'll warn you right now. It'll be virtually impossible to get me to crack. No one has been able to pry it from my lips."

Her gaze drifted to his mouth, her thoughts to his kisses.

No, no, no, she told herself. Not there. Not now.

"I like vinaigrette dressing," she said instead. "I can't wait to taste it."

He winked, and those kissable lips quirked up in a crooked grin.

She felt herself weakening, her thoughts flirting dangerously with memories of the past, of the night they'd made love until nearly dawn.

And that couldn't be good.

She struggled to find some generic words, something that would get their conversation and her thoughts back on track.

"What can I do to help?" she asked.

"I've got it all covered. So just come outside and watch me grill."

Okay. That was easy enough.

Once outdoors, he pulled up a patio chair, and she

took a seat. All the while, Woofer and Wags scrambled for her attention. The puppy jumped on her leg, and the dog nuzzled her hands, hoping for a scratch behind the ears.

"Hey, guys," Mike said to the dogs. "Give the lady a break."

She smiled, providing them each the attention they wanted. "It's kind of nice to know I was missed."

Mike had missed her, too. But he was glad she'd gotten out of the house and treated herself to a new hairstyle and a pedicure.

"Why don't you two go play," he told the dogs as he reached for the rubber ball he'd left on the porch railing a while back and hurled it to the back of the yard.

As the dogs raced to the corner of the fence, his words echoed the instructions his parents used to give him and the other children on nights the couple had sat down to watch a movie on television. Mike hadn't realized how difficult it must have been for his parents to juggle a love life around a houseful of rugrats, and his admiration for them grew.

"The dogs seem to be getting along much better now," Simone said.

"I agree. We should be able to start leaving them alone when we both have to work."

"Speaking of work," Simone said, "we had an interesting case the other night. A little boy found a stray bullet in his backyard and apparently decided to put it up his nose."

"Crazy kids. I've seen them put jelly beans and crayons up there. But a bullet? That must have been a bit tricky to get out."

They continued to talk about some of the interesting cases they'd had while working, as well as a couple of humorous situations they'd come across.

"My dad's birthday is Monday evening, so we're all going to get together at my parents' house. Sometimes, it's a bit of a zoo, but it's always entertaining. If you're free, I'd like you to go with me."

"Thanks, but I'll pass this time."

He nodded, focusing on the fact that she'd said *this time,* which implied she might be up for it in the future.

They made some more small talk, and before long, the chicken was done. After Mike placed it on a clean platter, they left the dogs in the yard to eat outside and went indoors to enjoy their own meal in the dining room.

Mike pulled out Simone's chair so she could sit down at the antique oak table. "I've got a bottle of merlot on the counter. If you give me a minute, I'll pour us each a glass."

"That's okay. I'd rather have water."

Was she still worried that the alcohol would lower her inhibitions and make her more susceptible to temptation? If so, she didn't need to be. He wasn't trying to go that route. He just wanted to set the mood and add a romantic touch.

He felt a bit funny drinking alone, but he didn't want the wine to go to waste. "I'll pour myself a glass, then. Do you want ice in your water?"

"Yes, please."

When he returned to the table, she seemed pensive, introspective. She bit down on her bottom lip, furrowed her brow and stared at her plate. He watched her for a while, intent upon keeping his mouth shut. But as they ate in silence, curiosity finally got the better of him.

"Who hurt you, Simone?"

She glanced up, her gaze snagging his. "What do you mean?"

"Who broke your heart? I get this feeling that a man did a real number on you, and you're not about to put yourself in that same position again."

She studied him for a moment, as though pondering what to say, what to reveal.

About the time he'd decided that she wasn't going to tell him, she said, "I dated this guy in college. I can't say that he did any real number on me. But he certainly made me aware of my deficiencies in a relationship."

Mike couldn't think of any flaws that she might have, other than refusing to let her feelings go and give love a chance. "The guy was a fool."

"No, Tom might have been brash and insensitive. But he pretty much got it right. He called me an ice queen, and it hurt—a lot. But I knew what he meant, and there wasn't anything I could do to change that."

"You weren't cold or unfeeling the night you and I slept together."

Her voice softened, even if her resolve didn't. "How about the next morning?"

Yeah. There was that.

She blotted her lips with a napkin, then pushed her plate aside. "I don't connect very well with people, Mike. I always hold back. And while I care about you— far more than is in my best interests—I can't give you and me the chance you want us to have."

"Why?" he asked, wanting to understand.

"Because my mother hated my father. Because she

never wanted me in the first place. Because she decided to be noble and carry me to term, which I appreciate, but she was hell-bent on keeping me when she should have given me to someone who would have loved me." Simone stood, picked up her plate, glass and silverware, then carried them into the kitchen, leaving Mike to second-guess what she'd just told him and to wonder what, if anything, she might have held back.

He, too, got to his feet and made his way to the kitchen with his own place setting.

"Hey," he said, sidling up to her as she filled the sink with hot, soapy water. "I didn't mean to pry."

She turned to face him. "I know. But it's best that you understand something. I didn't have the love that you had growing up. I'm not sure if you put any merit in child psychology, but I never bonded with my mom. I didn't learn to trust. Whenever I was hurt, no one gave a damn. So on the outside, I might look okay and act professionally. But on the inside, I'm scared and not so sure about things. And for that reason, I'm happier being alone."

Mike gently gripped her shoulders, the silky strands of her hair brushing against his knuckles. "You're a queen, but you're *not* made of ice. And I'll give you the time you need. Just don't shut me out because you have some wild-ass notion that you're looking out for *my* best interests."

Then he kissed her, long and hard and thorough.

Their tongues mated, their breaths mingled. Their hearts pounded out in need.

And when he was done, when there was a flush of arousal along her neck and chest, when her lips parted and her eyes widened, he excused himself for the evening and left her alone.

To think.

And, hopefully, to yearn for all that they could be together.

Chapter Eight

On Monday, Simone was asked to work an early shift to cover for Maureen Wiggins, an E.R. nurse who'd called in sick because of food poisoning.

So far, the morning had been relatively quiet, so while she took a lunch break, she carried a fantasy novel into the solarium, where she planned to spend some quiet time reading.

The solarium was a convenient place to take a break—and a cheerful one. An abundance of windows provided sunlight, as well as a view of the garden and the various elms, oaks and maples that had been growing on the hospital grounds for nearly forty years.

For the first time since the winter months had stripped the bushes bare, the roses had begun to bloom in a colorful array of buds and blossoms.

Because of the solitude and the view, the solarium

had become Simone's favorite place to steal a little reading time and escape into another world. Once inside, she planned to find a little alcove of cushiony chairs and make herself comfortable for the next twenty minutes or so. She'd even set the alarm on her watch so that she'd know when to end her break.

As she'd hoped, the solarium was nearly empty, other than a man talking on his cell phone in the corner.

She'd no more than glanced his way when she recognized Dr. Peter Wilder. Now that he was back in private practice, she didn't see him as often.

At first, she planned to ignore him and go about her business. But when she sensed he was having what appeared to be a serious, personal conversation with someone, Simone decided that it might be best if she left the room and let him speak in private.

"You're wrong, Anna," he said.

Simone easily surmised he was talking to his adopted sister.

Years ago, when Anna was an infant, she'd been left at the hospital by an unknown woman and adopted by Peter's parents. According to what Simone had gathered over the years by comments made to her by both Ella and Peter, their father, the late James Wilder, spent years trying to prove the family's love to Anna, which only created a strain between her and his other children.

To make matters worse, Anna had taken a position with NHC, and her family loyalty was in question.

Simone supposed, in some instances, adoptions might not work out the way everyone intended them to. And she'd have to keep that in mind.

For the first time since learning she was pregnant, she

realized that giving up the baby might not be the slam-dunk solution she'd been hoping for. That there were a lot of factors to consider.

But she supposed parenting, in general, was a difficult job—and not one to be taken lightly.

Peter glanced up, and when their gazes connected, Simone whispered, "Sorry." She motioned that she would leave him in private, but he shook his head, indicating that she didn't need to go.

Unfortunately, she felt uncomfortable either way.

"All right, I'll let you go. But do me a favor. Just try to see the family's side in this situation." Peter's lips tensed, then he slowly folded up his cell phone, ending the call without saying goodbye.

"I didn't mean to interrupt," Simone said.

"You didn't. We were hanging up anyway. Anna had a meeting to attend, so she said she'd talk to me later." Peter blew out a heavy sigh. "But I'm not so sure she'll call back. I'm afraid my sister is so removed from my life that she doesn't understand why I'm against the NHC takeover."

"I'm sorry to hear that." Simone thought highly of all the Wilders, and she sensed that the rift between Anna and her siblings was becoming more and more serious.

"If you had walked in a few minutes sooner, you would have heard a few heated words. I tried to explain how my dad felt about this hospital, how Ella, David and I feel, but Anna… Well, she just doesn't get it. I'm afraid that conversation we just had might have made things worse."

"Do you want to talk about it?" Simone didn't usually open up to her coworkers about her personal concerns and issues, but sometimes they found it easy to share with her. She suspected that was because she never took part in gossip or betrayed a confidence.

"There's really nothing to say." Peter got to his feet. "We've got some upcoming family weddings on the horizon, including my own. But I'm not even sure if Anna plans to attend any of them."

"It's tough when there's a rift in a family." Even when it was only a family of two, like Simone and her mother.

"You're right." As Peter approached Simone and headed for the door, he said, "The solarium is all yours now."

"Thanks."

As he left the sunlit room, Simone no longer felt like reading. Instead, she strode toward one of the windows and peered into the garden, noting the colorful signs of spring and renewal, the shoots of new growth and colorful blooms.

Peter's trouble with Anna only reminded her of the relationship she had with her mother.

It had been nearly a week, and her mom still hadn't returned her last call. But what else was new?

If the two of them had a normal relationship—she let the fantasy briefly play out in her mind—Simone would have called her mother to tell her about the baby. And if things had been different between them, she might have even looked forward to being a mother herself.

And perhaps she wouldn't be the least bit apprehensive about creating a family with Mike.

That night when she got home from work, Simone picked up the telephone and dialed her mother's number one last time. It wasn't all that unusual to be playing telephone tag with the woman.

But this time, Susan Garner answered on the third ring. "Hello?"

"Hey, Mom. It's me."

"Hi, Simone. You finally caught me at home. I'm afraid that I've been in and out a lot. I meant to return your call."

That was questionable.

"How are you doing?" Simone asked, disregarding the excuse given. "Cynthia called last week and told me you'd discovered a lump in your breast. I…I've been worried. And I wondered if there was anything I could do. If there were any questions you had."

"It was a bit scary for a while, but they did a biopsy and it came back benign."

"Well, good. That's great. And I imagine it's a big relief for you."

"Yes, it was." Susan blew out a sigh. "I'm really sorry Cynthia called you and bothered you with that. If it would have been…more serious…I would have called myself."

Would she have?

Somehow, Simone didn't think so. It was almost as if the two had never lived together, as if once Simone turned eighteen and could legally fly the coop, Susan's maternal responsibilities—what few she'd actually assumed—had ended.

"Well, I'm glad it all turned out okay," Simone said.

"Yes, everything is fine."

But it really wasn't. Not this conversation, not their relationship.

"I guess I'd better let you go, Mom. Be sure to tell Cynthia hello for me."

"I will. Good night, Simone."

The line disconnected.

Simone supposed the news should have been comforting, but she wanted to scream in frustration.

Why couldn't her relationship with her mother have been…normal? Or even just moderately dysfunctional?

In spite of the years Simone had spent building up a durable, Teflon hide and telling herself it really didn't matter, the disappointment and pain she'd experienced as a child and had locked away as an adolescent began to flood her heart with regret, and tears welled in her eyes.

Damn those pregnancy hormones.

And damn the past.

Woofer barked, then headed for the door, just moments before the bell sounded.

Oh, *great*. Now what? Simone hated to bother answering, especially all weepy-eyed and splotchy-faced. But neither did she want to hole up inside the house and pretend she wasn't home.

So she answered, albeit reluctantly, and found Mike on her porch. She could have sworn he'd told her he had an O'Rourke-family birthday party to attend. He must have decided to stop by on his way.

"Oh, honey," he said, reaching for the knob of the screen door without waiting to be invited inside.

She supposed he'd gotten used to making himself comfortable at her house. And she must have gotten used to having him around, too, because she grabbed Woofer's collar and used her foot to keep Wags from dashing outside. Then she stepped out of the way to let Mike in.

He gave each dog a detached greeting while focusing his attention on her. "What's the matter?"

Oh, God. She hated to spill her guts. But maybe, if she did, it would eventually make him realize why she wasn't the motherly type. Why the whole idea of home and family scared the heck out of her.

When Simone admitted that she'd finally talked to her mother about the lump she'd found, Mike wrapped his arms around her, probably assuming her tears were caused by bad news. "I'm so sorry."

Instead of immediately correcting him, she accepted his embrace and allowed herself a moment to savor his musky scent, his warmth, his compassion.

"Actually," she finally said, slowing drawing away from his arms, "the lump was benign."

"So you're crying from relief?"

"Yes and no. It's kind of complicated. It also hurts that my mother refused to return my calls, saying she didn't want to bother me with her problem."

"Maybe she was trying to protect you."

"If it were anyone else's mom, I might accept that. But not when it's mine."

He took her by the hand and led her to the sofa. "Why don't you sit down and talk to me about it."

It didn't feel right having the ugliness out in the open, but maybe it would be therapeutic in a sense. So she took a seat and waited for him to join her.

"I told you some of it already," she said. "About how my mom was cold and unloving."

He nodded. "I figured you'd held something back. You always do. But you don't need to do that with me."

She hoped he was right. "I knew that other kids had parents who played games with them. Moms and dads who asked how their day at school went, who tucked them in at night and listened to their prayers. But I never experienced anything like that. And no matter how hard I tried, I couldn't seem to connect on any level with my mother."

He didn't comment; he just continued to listen as she vented—something she wasn't used to doing.

"When I was a kid, I would have to change the channel whenever *The Wonderful World of Disney* was on television. It was too sad. I'd see commercials about Disneyland or Walt Disney World, with happy, loving families having the time of their lives. But I never even went to an amusement park. No visits to the petting zoo, no pony rides. None of the usual family experiences."

"I'm sorry that your childhood was so lousy."

"Me, too," she said. "But don't get me wrong. I never went without the material things. There was plenty of food. And I had regular health checkups. But sometimes my mom would glare at me. Or strike me for no reason."

"You were physically abused, too?" he asked.

"It's not like I was beaten. But I learned to stay out of my mom's reach."

While Mike continued to hold her hand, he brushed his thumb across her skin, soothing her, comforting her with the simplest touch. And she couldn't help but accept all he offered.

"I have a great mom," he said. "And I can't even imagine what I would have done or who I would have become without her."

He still didn't know the worst of it, Simone realized. He didn't know why her relationship with her mother had been so bad. Or why it still was. And so she decided to tell him what she hadn't told anyone else.

"When I was in the seventh grade, my mom told me to clean out the garage. And while I was moving some things around, I found a box of old photos and a diary. I knew her journal contained her private thoughts and that I shouldn't read it. But I'd always wanted to know my mom better, to understand what made her tick."

"And did you?"

"Yes. The early pages revealed a much different person than the one I'd known. She'd grown up in the sixties and had been happy and carefree. She used to write poetry. I guess you could say that she was… normal."

"When did that change?"

"When she was seventeen. By the time I got to the end of the diary, to the place where she'd finally quit writing, it all fell into place." Simone's fingers tightened around Mike's hands, then she slowly loosened them. She wasn't sure whether she wanted to cling to his touch or pull away.

His grip tightened, making the decision easier for her.

"My mom was raped, and I was the result."

Mike didn't respond, and she struggled not to peer at his face, not to try and read something in his expression. She'd just revealed the fact that she'd been the product of a violent act, not a loving one.

"My mom actually knew the guy and had gone out with him," she added. "So it would be classified as a date rape now. But back in the late sixties, when it happened, she felt that it was all her fault. And because I look like my father…"

"Did you know him?" Mike asked.

"No." She paused, thinking it best to explain. "Well,

my mom never said that I resembled him, and I never asked. But I don't look at all like her, so I can't help believing that each time she looked at me she was reminded of him, of what he'd done to her. And for that reason, she inadvertently—and subconsciously—took her anger and resentment out on me."

"You have no idea how sorry I am. For you, of course. But for her, too."

"Needless to say, this isn't something I'm proud of. But it's had an adverse effect on any relationship I've had. And that's why having a husband and children scares me to death. I don't want to hurt the people who depend upon me the most."

He seemed to ponder her words and her concern for a moment, then slowly shook his head. "No, that's not going to happen. For the past couple of years, I've watched you with your patients, young and old. And I've even seen you interact with the dogs, even when they're misbehaving. You'd never hurt anyone, intentionally or otherwise."

"I wish I could believe you, Mike. But I'm damaged goods."

He cupped her cheek. "You'll never be able to convince me of that. It's simply not true. I'm in love with you, Simone. And that's not going to change."

She wanted to believe him—she really did. But she couldn't take the chance.

What if he was wrong? What if she couldn't bond with the baby she was carrying?

Simone sat in the Walnut River OB/GYN waiting room, thumbing through a magazine and listening for her name to be called. She'd had blood drawn earlier, as ordered, and had already discussed insurance and financial obligations.

Now she was waiting for her first exam.

Last night, Mike had stayed at her house until she'd chased him off, telling him not to be late to his father's birthday party. She could tell he was reluctant to leave her alone, but she'd insisted she was fine.

And she was. She'd been dealing with her mom and the past for years.

Several times over the course of his visit, she'd been tempted to tell him about the baby. But she'd decided to wait until after seeing Dr. Kipper. After all, other than a little morning sickness and an occasional bout of light-headedness, she still didn't *feel* pregnant. Shouldn't she wait for some kind of confirmation?

As she sat in the cheerful waiting room, with its cream-colored walls and the lavender- and green-stenciled border, she couldn't seem to focus on any of the colorful ads or articles in her magazine.

Instead, she checked out the other patients, most of whom were visibly pregnant.

A blonde with a belly the size of a watermelon sat across from her, and she imagined herself big with child, her hands resting on her womb. Maybe she'd feel a little bump move by—a hand or a foot.

The dark-haired new mother to her left held a sleeping newborn in her arms. And, for a moment, Simone envisioned herself bringing the baby to an after-delivery checkup.

The door swung open, and someone else—a redhead—entered. She was about six months along and had a toddler with her. An older woman was only steps behind, and Simone suspected it was the grandmother.

Pregnant women should have the love and support of their mothers, which was another reason why Simone couldn't imagine keeping her baby. The only person she had to rely on was herself. But that was her reality, and she'd learned to accept it.

She wished she could say that her revelation to Mike about the details surrounding her conception and her childhood had been therapeutic. In a way, she supposed it had been. At least it was out in the open now.

When the nurse, a fifty-something blonde with a warm smile, called Simone's name from the doorway, she stood, leaving the magazine on the table next to her, and let the matronly woman lead her toward the exam rooms.

They stopped by the scale, then went through the usual routine of taking her blood pressure and checking her pulse. After being given a plastic cup and pointed in the direction of the restroom, she provided them with a urine sample.

It was an interesting twist to be a patient rather than a medical professional for a change. And she wasn't sure that she liked it.

Next, she undressed and donned the backless hospital-style gown that everyone hated, then climbed up on the exam table. Fortunately, she didn't have to wait long for Dr. Kipper to come in, accompanied by the nurse.

"I've gone over the lab work," the tall, slender obstetrician said. "Everything looks good."

The following pelvic exam was also normal.

"Since you're over thirty-five," Dr. Kipper said as he reached for her hand and helped her to a sitting position on the table, "I'm going to suggest an amniocentesis at sixteen weeks."

He went on to explain the procedure and the risks, then answered all her questions.

She mentioned being light-headed a time or two and actually fainting once, although she hadn't eaten since the night before. He told her that it wasn't uncommon and suggested that she keep her blood sugar level steady by having more frequent and smaller meals. He also told her that a sudden change in blood pressure could also be the cause. And that she should change positions slowly.

"Let me know if the fainting or dizziness becomes frequent," he said.

"All right. I will."

He wrote something in her chart, then glanced up. "Are you taking any vitamins?"

"Just the generic variety I normally take."

He dug through the cupboard and found a couple of packets. "I've got a sample of the prenatal vitamins I'd like you to start taking instead. I've got them in either pink or blue. Do you have a preference?"

"No, it doesn't matter." Yet thoughts of pink had her thinking about sugar and spice and everything nice, while blue brought on a reminder of frogs, snails and puppy-dog tails.

Would Mike have a preference?

No, she snapped at herself. Don't even go there.

"I'd like to see you back in three weeks," Dr. Kipper said.

She nodded, feeling a bit robotic.

When the doctor and his nurse left her alone in the room, she removed the drafty gown and got dressed.

Next, she stopped at the checkout window, where she made a payment.

On the way out of the office, she spotted Millie seated in the waiting room, near a potted palm.

Millie looked up from the magazine she was reading, her gaze landing on Simone. "Hey! Fancy meeting you here."

Simone had thought the exact thing. And for a moment, she hoped that Millie was here for the same reason, that God had listened to her prayers, and she'd somehow become pregnant.

"How about that," Simone said.

Millie set the magazine in her lap. "I'm here for my yearly Pap smear. How about you?"

Simone didn't have the heart to tell her she was pregnant. And for more reasons than one.

If she miscarried, which was a possibility, especially in the first three months, and Millie was expecting to adopt the baby, it would be an unnecessary disappointment and heartbreak for her friend.

And secondly, she wasn't ready to let the cat out of the bag.

Or is it more than that? a small inner voice asked. *Are you trying to hold on to the baby, as well as the news?*

Simone quickly shook off the stray thought.

"Pap smears aren't something I look forward to, but they're very important," she told her friend, tottering on the truth and a lie of omission.

"I know." Millie scanned the room and zeroed in on a petite brunette who looked to be about nine months pregnant and ready to pop. When her gaze returned to Simone, her eyes glistened with unshed tears.

Simone's heart went out to the woman who would make a wonderful mother. Again she thought about giving her baby to Millie and Fred. If she were to do that, the child would undoubtedly grow up happy and loved.

Yet a sudden sense of uneasiness settled over her when she thought about handing over her child, a selfish response that left her with a nagging sense of guilt.

Simone didn't have any business even thinking about keeping the baby.

So what had caused the momentary change of heart?

Chapter Nine

Last week, Mike had invited Simone out to dinner to Rafael's, a classy restaurant in downtown Walnut River, complete with candles, white linen tablecloths and the best chef and service for miles around.

For a woman who'd never had a romantic bone in her body, she was sorely tempted to don that only-worn-once black dress she owned—or maybe buy a new one—and let him sweep her off to a dreamy dinner for two. She could almost imagine herself sitting across a candlelit table from the most handsome man in all of Walnut River, a young, dark-haired hunk who clearly had eyes for her.

Little by little, Mike had been whittling away at her resolve to remain single and unattached, which had protected her well over the years. And at times, she found herself leaning toward sentiment rather than wisdom.

So, she'd declined—with more reluctance than she cared to admit.

Then, on Tuesday, he'd suggested they each take some vacation time and go to Martha's Vineyard for a few days. He'd said he wanted to take her to the Cape before the tourist season kicked in.

She'd found the idea strangely appealing and the thought of the possible sleeping arrangements…intriguing.

But again she'd refused.

She didn't think it would be wise to leave the hospital when it looked as though the allegations of insurance fraud were being investigated. Nor did she know how long she could fight her attraction to a man whose perseverance was both frustrating and flattering.

And now, Mike stood on her front porch with a bouquet of roses in one hand and two white bags in the other. Apparently, he was at it again—trying to make more of their relationship than it really was.

Still, as much as she hated to admit it, she'd begun to enjoy Mike's company, so she invited him in.

The first thing he did, after handing her the flowers, was to kick off his shoes by the door. "If you'll put those roses in some water, I'll get everything set up."

"What do you mean?"

He tossed her a boyish grin that knocked her heart on end. "I'm setting the mood. Our food will taste better this way. We're going to sit on the floor and use chopsticks instead of forks."

She watched as he placed the bags that boasted the red pagoda logo of the Tokyo Palace on the coffee table.

Then he removed two cushions from the couch and set them on the floor.

Too cute, she thought, heading for the kitchen. And far too charming for his own good.

Hers, too, she realized. Sometimes, in spite of their opposing goals and dreams, she found herself weakening toward him and wondering, What if…

And not just sexually speaking.

While she stood at the sink and filled a vase with water, she glanced out into the yard, where Woofer and Wags lay in the shade of an elm tree. The dogs had grown comfortable with each other in the past week or so.

The same could be said for Simone and Mike, she supposed.

She had to admit that she admired his spirit, as well as his thoughtfulness, and a solid friendship was clearly developing.

Would that make telling him about the baby easier or more difficult?

She couldn't be sure.

Maybe she ought to just get it over with while they ate dinner—a game plan which seemed wise, especially after the dream she'd had last night. She'd awakened in the midst of it and found the image so unsettling that she'd climbed out of bed at 4:00 a.m. and put on a pot of water for a cup of tea.

In her dream, she'd held a baby girl, a sweet bundle of flannel and lace who'd had Mike's black hair and green eyes. The smiling cherub had settled comfortably in Simone's arm and turned a new mommy's heart inside out—until the helpless babe began to cry.

A sense of panic had settled in, waking Simone from her sleep.

She feared that dreams like that might start hounding her subconscious until she finally told Mike she was pregnant and was able to put it all behind her.

Mike might have taken her past in stride, but he couldn't convince her that she hadn't come away from it unscathed.

And although he wasn't worried about how she'd handle marriage and a family, she wasn't ready to gamble with a child's psyche.

Before the water threatened to spill out of the vase, she shut off the spigot. Next she cut off about an inch or so from the stems of the roses and arranged them carefully. When she carried the red buds back into the living room, Mike appeared to have everything planned just so.

"Do you care where I put these?" she asked.

"Not at all."

In that case, she placed them in the center of her antique china hutch, then took a seat on one of the sofa cushions Mike had placed on the floor and studied the Japanese feast he'd spread out on the coffee table. He'd picked up wontons, California roll, a variety of sashimi, miso soup, steamed rice and chicken teriyaki.

"It looks good," she said.

"Thanks. Why don't you take a seat while I get us something to drink."

"All right."

"What would you like?"

"Water sounds good to me."

When he returned from the kitchen with both glasses,

he placed one in front of her and the other on his side of the table. Then he took his seat.

"How about some sashimi?" he asked. "I've got ahi and salmon."

"I'll pass." She wasn't sure what the rules were on eating raw fish when a woman was pregnant, so until she had a chance to read up on it, she thought it was best to decline.

He took a sip of his ice water. "I stocked some beer and wine in the fridge last time I was here. But I decided not to offer you any. I didn't want you to think I was trying to ply you with alcohol."

"Why would I think that?" she asked.

"I don't know. Because I've offered you wine a couple of times. Of course, to be honest, I wouldn't mind seeing you loosen up some."

She bristled, sensing what he was about to say.

"You hold yourself back," he went on to explain. "And I understand why you do. But there was a warm glow about you on the night we attended Dr. Wilder's party, and you had a happy glimmer in your eyes."

"That's because I was tipsy." And she'd be darned if she'd let that happen again.

"No, I noticed it when you reached for your first glass of champagne. I'm not sure you'd even taken a sip, but either way, I saw a side of you I hadn't seen before, and it was nice."

"That side of me doesn't really exist."

"I disagree. I think you let that woman out of her cage every now and again."

For a moment, Simone was transported back to her college days. Back to when Tom broke up with her, saying pretty much the same thing. *You need to loosen up, Simone. You're strung too tight. You've built walls around yourself. And whenever anyone tries to get too close, you shut them out and turn on the deep freeze.*

Tom's words had stunned her to silence, and she'd felt herself recoil into an emotional fetal position, her heart frosting over and preparing for the worst.

Dammit. He'd slammed the palm of his hand down on the console of his car. *There you go again, Simone, shutting me out. You're an ice queen.*

Mike hadn't said those exact words, but his meaning was clear. And his thoughts had undoubtedly drifted in the same direction as Tom's had that long-ago day on the way home from the shore.

"Is something wrong?" Mike asked.

Yes, something was wrong. They'd created a child. A baby she couldn't keep. And she was going to have to level with him—*now*. While he was reminded of the woman she really was.

And who she wasn't.

Oh, God, she pleaded, hoping The Man Upstairs cared enough to listen to her these days, that he cared enough to help her get the words out and set things to rights. *I've got to tell him. And then I need to stand firm.*

She raked a hand through the strands of her hair, then blew out a ragged breath. "There's something you need to know."

Mike, who was fiddling with his chopsticks, placed them on his paper plate and gazed at her. "What's that?"

"I'm pregnant."

His brow twitched, and his jaw dropped. "You're kidding."

"Believe me, I may not have the best sense of humor in the world, but there's no way I'd joke about something like that."

"Is it mine?" His expression went from disbelief to *well-duh* in less than a millisecond. "Sorry. Of course it's mine. I didn't mean to… Wow."

Yeah. *Wow.*

"That's actually…cool," he finally said, his initial shock morphing into an easy grin. "It's a bit of a surprise, but I'm perfectly okay with it."

Simone wasn't sure what she'd been expecting him to say. Exactly that, she supposed.

But apparently, he hadn't been listening to her. Didn't he get it?

"Well, *I'm* not okay with it," she admitted. "And I think it's best for everyone involved if I give the baby up for adoption."

As Simone's cold hard solution hung in the air like the courthouse sentence of a convicted felon, Mike wanted to lash back, to argue. Yet he knew her well enough to keep his mouth shut and try to make some sense of this. To try to wrap his mind around it and form another game plan.

Damn.

Simone was pregnant.

With *his* baby.

For some crazy reason, he couldn't stop a goofy smile from curling the edges of his mouth.

Their lovemaking had created a child.

Mike adored his nieces and nephews—seven of them and still counting. How he'd like to see his own son or daughter join its cousins in a game of hide-and-seek or freeze tag.

His grin broadened—until the realization that she'd wanted to give up their kid shoved it aside.

Was she just trying to feel him out? To test his reaction? Women did that sometimes.

"You know," he said, "I've never made any secret about my feelings for you. And while I wasn't in a big rush to get married or have kids, that's not something we ought to put off."

"And I've made no secret about my fears," she countered. "I'm not mommy material. Haven't you been listening to me?"

Yes, but he'd hoped to change her mind.

In fact, he still did. He just hadn't counted on something like this happening—at least not this soon. But just because the timing might make a pregnancy a bit inconvenient didn't mean the baby would be a complication.

Hell, Mike could see himself getting used to the idea in no time at all.

He picked up his chopsticks and began to eat, even though his appetite had fizzled in the pit of his stomach and he was merely poking at his chicken.

Hers must have done the same thing, because she picked at her food, too.

They ate in silence until he felt compelled to argue his case one more time. "You can't convince me that you don't have feelings for me, too."

"I told you that I do. And more than I should."

"Our lovemaking was off the charts," he added. "We couldn't be any more sexually compatible."

"I agree. But great sex isn't enough of a basis for marriage. Neither is parenthood."

What was up with her attitude about the baby?

Their baby.

She could have been blindsided by the news, he supposed. And didn't pregnant women's hormones play havoc with them? "All I'm saying is that we need to give ourselves some time to sort through this."

She pushed her plate aside, then dropped her used napkin on top. "Time isn't going to change anything. You're looking for Mrs. Right, and I'm clearly not that woman."

He tried to tell himself to go easy on her at a time like this. She'd told him about growing up with a mother who hadn't shown her any love. And on top of that, she had to be struggling with a multitude of changes in her body.

Maybe she was also considering all the obvious adjustments a baby—and a husband, if Mike had his way—would require her to make when it came to the life she'd created for herself.

But the news of her pregnancy, along with her thoughts of adoption, had unbalanced him.

"You know," she said, "I'm really tired and probably ought to turn in for the night."

Was she? Or was she just trying to get rid of him?

"Okay," he said. "I'll take off. I'm on duty tomorrow, too. But maybe we can talk more about this the next day."

"There's not much to say."

"Oh, I think there is." Yet something twisted in his gut, something that made him want to shove his plate aside, too.

Damn. Why was her first thought to give up their baby?

If she insisted, there was no way in hell that Mike would stand for it. And she had to have his agreement, didn't she?

All his carefully laid plans had begun to unravel at the edges.

Ever since the night of Dr. Wilder's party, he'd been telling her that he'd give her the time she needed. That she'd soon realize the two of them were made for each other. But if she didn't give him something to go on soon, he was going to back off. Hell, his ego, as strong and cocky as it sometimes was, couldn't take the constant brush-off.

She walked him to the door, and while he thought about kissing her senseless, he brushed his lips across her brow instead.

"Sleep tight," he said.

"You, too."

Yeah, right. He had a lot to think about, a lot to keep him awake.

He tried to remind himself how good sex had been. How hot their kisses were.

But Mike was only human.

And the truth was, his heart could only take so much.

The next morning, at the station, Mike watched a gin game that had grown pretty intense, but his mind was on the bombshell—actually two of them—he'd received the night before.

Simone was having his baby.

And she wanted to give it up.

At least, she hadn't decided upon an abortion, which made him feel better.

He understood that she might have wished her mother would have given her to parents who would have loved and appreciated her. But this was different.

Mike wanted the baby. And deep in his heart, he believed Simone wanted it, too.

Preferring to stew in his own thoughts and suffer alone, he got to his feet and walked out of the station.

When footsteps sounded behind him, he turned to see his partner, Leif Johnson, a stocky redhead with blue eyes and a quick wit.

Leif knew how Mike felt about Simone, but then again, a lot of people probably did. Mike never did try to hide his feelings.

Of course, that didn't mean he was the kind of man who kissed and told.

"Hey," Leif said. "You look like you're a million miles away."

"I guess I am."

"Would getting it off your chest help?"

Leif had known that Mike had taken Simone home after Dr. Wilder's party, but that's all he knew. Mike hadn't leveled with anyone about what he and Simone had shared that night. But now that Simone had him second-guessing himself and his feelings, he wasn't sure about anything anymore.

Mike leaned against the outside wall of the building and crossed his arms. "Do you remember when they christened the hospital library in honor of James Wilder? And the cocktail party Peter Wilder invited us to?"

"Yeah."

Normally, paramedics didn't get included in those kinds of hospital social events. But Mike and Leif had been on duty the night James Wilder suffered the fatal heart attack. And they'd tried valiantly—but unsuccessfully—to save his life. As a result, the two had been added to the guest list.

"I gave Simone a ride home that night," Mike said.

"Yeah, I remember." Leif smiled. "She looked like maybe she'd had a little too much to drink."

"Well, one thing led to another and…" Mike blew out a loaded sigh.

"No kidding?" Leif grinned, knowing how much Mike cared for Simone and immediately making the appropriate jump. "Are you two still seeing each other?"

"Not like that. She says she just wants to be friends."

"Hey, that's life. I've had my share of women tell me the same thing. That is, until Linda and I hooked up."

Leif was dating a kindergarten teacher he'd met when her class had come to the fire station for a field trip. Leif didn't kiss and tell, either, but Mike knew that they'd been sleeping together.

One morning about a month ago, Leif hadn't come home the night before. He'd apparently left his headlamps on and couldn't get his car to start. So he'd had to call Mike and ask for a ride to work.

Linda seemed like a nice woman, and Mike hoped they'd be happy.

"So what's the problem?" Leif asked. "Just cut bait and run."

"I would, but I can't help believing that Simone and I are meant for each other. But she's so…" Mike didn't want to go into too much personal detail. "So damn set in her ways."

Leif placed a hand on Mike's back. "I know it hurts,

man. But you can't chase after a woman who clearly isn't interested. There are stalking laws and all that."

Mike clucked his tongue. "I'm not a stalker. And I know when a woman isn't interested. If I truly believed it, I'd back way off."

"So she's given you reason to believe there's hope?"

"Yeah." She'd admitted that she cared for him. And he couldn't help believing her, especially when he remembered the way she'd looked at him when they'd made love—talk about someone wearing their heart on their sleeve.

At three in the morning, she'd lost that tipsy glow, and it had been replaced by something else. Something laden with an emotion a man couldn't mistake for friendship or simple desire.

But maybe he'd read her wrong.

Maybe she didn't have the right kind of feelings for him, and he'd been pushing her too hard.

"Chasing after her just isn't cool," Leif added. "It makes you look needy."

His partner had a point. Mike had made himself too available. It might be best if he backed off.

"Linda has a couple of friends. They're both single and hot. Without a doubt, either of them would drop everything to go out on a date with you."

The trouble was, Mike didn't want to go out with anyone other than Simone. And he sure as hell didn't want to go out with anyone when Simone was having his baby.

Damn.

His baby.

Their baby.

"What you need is a diversion," Leif said. "And have

I got the woman for you. Her name is Christy, and she's about five-two. She's a school librarian, but don't think that means she's prim and proper. She's bright, well read and funny."

Mike needed to get his mind off Simone, all right. But not by dating another woman. "I may back off with Simone. But I'm not ready to go out with anyone else."

"Why not?"

"It's complicated."

"Suit yourself," Leif said. "But promise me you'll stop pining for a woman who doesn't want you."

While Mike could see the value in that advice, he couldn't completely give up on Simone.

Not just yet.

But how could a woman be so stubborn?

Mike still hoped to change her mind, but he was beginning to have his doubts. He suspected that was why the seed of a plan B began to form. A plan that he'd implement if backed into a corner.

A move that could end any dream Mike had of him and Simone creating a family together.

Chapter Ten

After Mike left Simone's house, she'd cleaned up the dinner mess. It had been quick and easy; she'd just packed up the leftovers in plastic ware before refrigerating them, then thrown away the take-out bags and cartons.

But she suspected she'd made a mess out of her friendship with Mike. And if she chose to do something about that, it wouldn't be as easy to straighten up.

She'd shut him out by suggesting he go home, which she was prone to do whenever things got emotionally involved. But for once in her life, she hadn't been especially happy about being left alone.

After feeding the dogs and getting them situated in the kitchen for the night, she'd showered and put on her favorite pink flannel gown, then climbed into bed. The sheets had been laundered earlier that day, which, under normal conditions, meant she could expect a good night's sleep.

Instead, her mind refused to shut down and continued to go over their dinnertime conversation again and again. She'd kept trying to figure out a better way she could have handled it, but hadn't been able to.

Mike had a different spin on the pregnancy situation than she had. And he had a different solution, too.

Unfortunately, she'd had to work the next day, and as a result, had arrived at the hospital a bit distracted by lack of sleep and thoughts of Mike and the baby. Of course, she'd tried to shake them off the best that she could.

Now she sat behind the desk at the nurses' station in the E.R., reading the orders one of the residents had written on a patient's chart.

There'd been a traffic accident on the interstate about an hour earlier, and a seventeen-year-old passenger in one of the cars had been sent to X-ray with a possible broken arm and collarbone.

"Is that the Stephens chart?" Ella asked.

"Yes, it is." Simone handed her the paperwork, pleased Ella had been the orthopedic surgeon who'd been called in to treat the teen's injury.

Ella looked the chart over, then asked, "When is he due back from radiology?"

"It shouldn't be much longer."

Ella nodded. When she finished perusing the chart, she glanced across the desk at Simone. "Did you hear that the state attorney general's office is sending an investigator to do a preliminary investigation about possible insurance fraud?"

"When?"

"Within the next few days, I've heard." Ella set the chart aside.

"I don't like the sound of that."

"Neither do I."

"It's so unfair," Simone added. "Walnut River General might keep its patients longer than most hospitals, but it's not an attempt to defraud insurance companies. It's because we don't believe in sending patients home early just to keep the costs down."

"They won't uncover anything fraudulent. But from what I understand, the investigator is going to interview anyone who might have information about the alleged fraud. That means doctors, nurses and the administrative staff."

"That will cast suspicion on everyone, which won't be good for morale. Besides, I'm not looking forward to having a stranger snooping around here. Not that I expect them to uncover anything." Simone chuffed. "You know, we have enough to worry about these days. Since the board rejected NHC's last offer, the takeover attempts could become hostile."

"I'm glad my father isn't alive to see what's going on. He loved this hospital."

Ella didn't mention it, but Simone wondered how James Wilder would have felt about his adopted daughter, Anna, working for the conglomerate that wanted to take over Walnut River General.

Not pleased, Simone decided.

"Are you going to attend the retirement party for Henry Weisfield on Sunday afternoon?" Ella asked.

Simone wasn't up for another party/dress-up affair.

But she'd have to at least make an appearance. "I may stop by for a few minutes."

"Long enough to have a glass of champagne?" Ella asked. "J.D. and I are having a private celebration." She grinned. "It's now official. He'll be taking over Henry's position."

"That's great news, but I'm afraid I've given up drinking champagne. It doesn't sit well with my resolve to remain unattached."

"Maybe you ought to drink more of it," Ella said with a smile. "You had a lovely glow that night we re-christened the hospital library."

Yep. Wrapped in Mike's arms, Simone had smoldered until dawn that night. And now she had a *pregnancy glow* to look forward to.

"By the way," Ella said, "I saw Mike walking Woofer and the puppy the other day. It looks like you two have figured out a shared-custody arrangement."

Simone's heart sank to the pit of her stomach, causing a wave of nausea to render her speechless.

"What's the matter?" Ella asked. "Is that a touchy subject?"

"It's just that…" Simone blew out a wobbly breath. Normally, she'd keep news like her pregnancy a secret. But it was going to be common knowledge as soon as she started showing.

Besides, she and Ella had become closer in the past few months.

Simone hadn't been sure how or when it had happened. She'd always respected Ella, but lately she'd come to enjoy her company, too.

So, she scanned the immediate area, checking to see

who might be listening in. When she was convinced their conversation was private, she cleared her throat. "Well, there's the dog thing, yes. But when you mentioned shared custody, I…well, it hit a little too close to home."

"What do you mean?"

"I'm pregnant."

Ella sat back in her chair, the springs creaking in protest. "Oh, Simone… Does Mike know?"

"Yes." Simone blew out a sigh. "And to make matters worse, Mike and I have opposing beliefs on what would be best for everyone involved."

"He wants to…?" Ella merely looked at Simone, prompting an answer she might have normally kept to herself.

"He wants to get married and live happily ever after."

"And you don't?"

"I can't, Ella."

Footsteps sounded, and both women grew silent. Simone was glad to refocus her thoughts on work.

If her mind would only cooperate.

Simone had just arrived home from the market and was unloading her car when Mike drove up in his Jeep. She watched as he got out of the vehicle and approached.

He was wearing a pair of faded jeans, a white polo shirt and an unreadable expression. Sheepish? Pensive? Intense?

"If I help you put away your groceries," he said, "will you take a ride with me?"

"Where?"

"It's a surprise."

A part of her was glad to know he hadn't shut her out

of his life completely, and since it was rare that anyone had a surprise for her, she was also curious.

"All right," she said.

Minutes later, after they'd placed the frozen food in the freezer and the eggs and dairy products in the fridge, they stacked the pasta, rice and canned goods in the pantry.

"Okay," Mike said. "Let's go."

Simone glanced down at the clothes she was wearing—a pair of black slacks, which had a little more room in the waistband and just seemed to feel better than her jeans these days. She also had on a lime-green, scoop-necked top with an empire waist. The shirt was stylish, yet she realized it looked a bit like a maternity blouse without all the extra material. Not that she needed a new wardrobe yet.

"Should I change my clothes?" she asked.

"No, you look great." The warmth in his grin convinced her of his sincerity.

So she grabbed her purse and, after locking the house, followed him to his Jeep. Before climbing into the passenger side, she again asked, "Where are we going?"

"Just for a drive. I want to show you something." He opened the door and waited for her to get in.

He always behaved like a gentleman around her, and she decided there was a lot about Mike to admire. A lot to love.

A wistful ache settled in her chest, and she wished she could let go of her fears and accept his optimism. He made it all sound so simple, when she was a realist and knew that having a relationship with him—at least, the kind he wanted and deserved—would be anything but easy for her.

After she slid into her seat, he closed the door, circled the vehicle and climbed into the driver's side.

Minutes later, they were driving through the tree-shaded streets of Riverdale.

She suspected he wanted to show her the Dennison place, or rather the home he'd just placed an offer on. And if truth be told, she'd like to see it, too.

After he turned onto Maple and passed the first curve in the road, she realized that's exactly what he had in mind.

He pulled along the curb in front of a three-story, pale yellow Victorian-style home with white gingerbread trim and shut off the ignition.

The house needed paint and some fix-it work done, but the place had enormous potential.

"The owners agreed to rent it to me before the close of escrow," he said. "So I moved in early this morning. Come on. I want to show you the inside, as well as the yard."

As he led her to the house, she realized that the lawn had been freshly mowed, trimmed and watered. She also saw that the sidewalk and porch had been swept clean and washed down. She suspected Mike had been eager to get to work on his new place.

Or had he wanted to make a good impression on her?

He unlocked the front door and waited for her to enter. Once they were inside the house, he pointed out the hardwood floors, a redbrick fireplace that bore smoke and soot stains from years of use and a curved banister that led upstairs.

The walls had been covered in a faded blue-and-yellow floral wallpaper that Simone suspected was part of the original decor. If not, it had been a part of the house for years.

There were five bedrooms upstairs and one down. It seemed like a lot of square footage for a single man. Still, she could understand why a guy like him might want to tackle a big renovation, as this was bound to be.

The kitchen, with its retro-style appliances and scarred gray linoleum, needed to be remodeled. The bathrooms—three of them—did, too. Yet there was a charm to the place, and she truly believed Mike had lucked out when it went on the market.

"The house is wonderful, Mike. You're really going to enjoy refurbishing it."

"I know. And I can't wait to get started." He placed a hand on her back and ushered her through the kitchen to the service porch, then out the door. The back lawn, like the one in front, had been newly mowed. A sprinkler had been turned on and was raining some much-needed water on the dried-out blades of grass.

She suspected, before long, it would soon be a lovely shade of green.

On the other hand, the shrubs, trees and bushes were in desperate need of a trim, and the flower beds could stand some attention from someone with a green thumb.

"The yard still looks like a jungle," Mike said, "but with some work, I ought to be able to whip it into shape before you know it."

"You're going to get lost inside of this old place alone. Are you planning to fix it up, then turn around and resell it?"

For a moment, his smile faltered, and his excitement

waned. But just for a beat. "I plan to get married and fill it up with kids."

She suspected he'd been thinking about her and knew she would have to disappoint him again.

Yet the thought of him finding a younger woman and creating a family with someone else twisted her heart in an unnatural direction.

Rather than deal with the emotional discomfort of either option, she clung to the silence.

Mike walked to the side of the house, where he turned off the sprinkler. "I'll take Wags with me when I drop you off."

She ought to be happy to have one less dog, but she'd gotten attached to the little scamp. Of course, she didn't dare mention anything like that.

"Would it be okay with you if I picked up Woofer sometimes and brought him over to visit Wags?" Mike asked.

"Sure." The dogs had become much closer these days, and she suspected they'd miss each other.

Shared custody, an inner voice whispered, bringing to mind that unsettling term again. But she quickly shrugged it off.

Mike grabbed some kind of electrical, long-handled tool that had been leaning near the back porch. "Do you mind if we make a stop before I take you home and pick up Wags? I have to return this edger."

She didn't mind. Nor was she in any hurry to get rid of that scruffy puppy with big, brown eyes. She was going to miss the little guy who met her at the door or the gate with a yappy bark and an I-need-you whine.

After locking up the house, they headed for his Jeep.

And moments later, they were on the road. Mike drove along Lexington to the other side of Walnut River and turned onto Cambridge Court.

When he parked in front of a white stucco house with redbrick trim, she asked, "Who lives here?"

"My folks. I borrowed the edger from my dad."

All the way across town? It would have been easier to drop her off at her house first. Of course, he also wanted to pick up Wags. Maybe he didn't want to take Wags to his parents' house.

Yet something told her he might have an ulterior motive for bringing her with him. Had he come up with a phony excuse to force her to meet his parents?

"Come in with me," he said, reaching for the door handle.

Simone stiffened. "Why?"

"Because I'd like to introduce you to my mom and dad."

Had he told them about the baby? About his plans to marry her?

A sense of panic settled over her, and she couldn't seem to move.

"You can wait in the car if you want," he said. "But you don't need to do that. Just come inside and say hello. We can leave whenever you want to."

Her stance didn't soften in the least. "Did you tell them about the baby?"

If he had, she wasn't sure what she'd do.

"No," he said, "I haven't said a word to anyone. Not even to Leif. But that's not because I didn't want to."

He seemed to have backed her into a corner, and while she didn't feel like going through the how-do-you-do and the nice-to-meet-you motions, she un-hooked her seat belt and got out of the Jeep.

As she strode up the walkway, she tugged at the hemline on her blouse, now really hoping it didn't look like a maternity top.

When Mike rang the bell, he didn't wait for anyone to answer. Instead, he swung open the door for Simone and called out, "Hey, it's me. Is anyone home?"

"Mikey!" a woman's voice said. "Come on in. I'm in the kitchen."

As Mike led Simone through the house, she couldn't help looking around the modest but cozy living room, with its display of family photos on the mantel of a brick fireplace.

The warm aroma of sugar and spice filled the air and suggested someone was baking. As Mike led her to a small but functional kitchen, the mouthwatering scent grew stronger.

Sure enough, she'd been right. A salt-and-pepper-haired woman wearing oven mitts was placing a cake onto an open breadboard to cool off. When she straightened, a loose curl flopped onto her forehead.

"Looks like we arrived just in time," Mike said to Simone. "My mom is the best cook in New England, if not the entire country."

Mrs. O'Rourke caught Simone's eye and grinned. "My kids are biased. But I do love to cook. And there's usually something on the stove or in the oven. I never know when one of them will come home. And when they do, they often have several friends with them." She removed the mitts and reached out a hand to Simone. "Hi. I'm Rhonda O'Rourke. And while you're welcome to have some carrot cake, it'll taste better after it cools and I can whip up the sour-cream frosting."

Simone took the older woman's hand in greeting as Mike introduced them.

"It's nice to meet you," Simone said.

"We won't be staying long," Mike added. "I just brought Dad's edger back."

"It's too bad that you can't stay," Rhonda said. "I've got some iced tea and leftover apple cobbler I can feed you. That is, if your father didn't get into it while I was at the market earlier this morning. He's got such a sweet tooth."

"I don't know about Simone," Mike said, "but I could probably be coaxed into staying long enough to have some coffee and cobbler. And speaking of Dad, where is he?"

"Outside." Rhonda brushed at the errant curl with the back of her hand. "He's working on the new gazebo. It's nearly done."

"My dad retired after forty years as a police officer," Mike told Simone. "And ever since he left the department, he's taken an interest in the yard."

"Actually," Rhonda said, "he's always liked working with plants and flowers, but when our children were young, it seemed as though every kid in the neighborhood used to hang out at our house."

Mike cupped his hand around his mouth as though he meant to whisper, yet he kept his voice loud enough for his mom to hear. "Our friends all wanted to play here because of all the cookies and brownies they used to get."

Rhonda laughed, a warm, hearty lilt that a person could get used to hearing. "Okay, so I used to like knowing where my kids were at all times. And I wasn't beyond bribing them and their friends."

"Aha!" Mike said. "And here I thought you spent so much time in the kitchen because you loved to cook and bake."

Rhonda crossed her arms and grinned. "A mom's gotta do what a mom's gotta do."

Even Simone found herself smiling.

"So," Mike added, "with five of us kids living here, the doors and gates were swinging open and closed repeatedly."

"That's true. And poor Sam couldn't seem to do much in the yard except mow. The kids trampled any flowers or shrubs he tried to plant."

"So now that we're finally adults, he's making up for lost time."

"You ought to see the new rose garden." Rhonda pointed to a vase on the kitchen table, where a bouquet of flowers in shades of red, yellow and pink was displayed.

"Come on," Mike said to Simone. "I'll introduce you to my dad."

"Will you excuse me?" Simone asked Rhonda.

"Of course. I'll put on a pot of coffee and dish up the cobbler while you're outside."

Simone followed Mike as he led her to the sliding glass door. Through the window, she could see a lovely backyard.

Mr. O'Rourke, a stocky silver-haired man wearing a pair of khaki shorts, a bright yellow shirt and a green baseball cap, had his back to the house and was stooped over, pulling weeds from around the base of a rosebush bearing red buds.

When Mike pushed open the sliding door and stepped onto the patio, the older man looked up and grinned.

"Hey, Pop." Mike placed a hand on Simone's back as he escorted her across the lawn. "I brought your edger back."

The man's grin stretched into a broad smile. "Looks like you brought more than a lawn tool."

Mike chuckled. "Yep. This is Simone Garner, one of the nurses at Walnut River General." He then went on to introduce her to his father.

"I'd shake hands," Sam O'Rourke said, "but I'm afraid that would get you all dirty."

"Your wife was right," Simone said. "That's a lovely rose garden."

"Thanks. It's coming along nicely, although I'm still learning how to take care of it properly." Sam reached into his hip pocket and pulled out a pair of clippers. Then he cut off a blood-red bud, leaving the stem long. He snipped off the thorns before handing it to her. "Here you go, Simone. If you put this in water, it'll bloom for days. And the fragrance will surprise you."

"Thank you." She took the rose and sniffed the blossom. Sam was right; it smelled wonderful.

"You might want to come inside and wash up," Mike said. "Mom's putting on some coffee and cutting into the cobbler."

"That little woman is a real prize, but I gotta tell you, I've put on twenty-five pounds since my retirement." Sam patted his stomach, which hung over his belt. "But I'm not going to worry about that until Monday, when I start my new diet."

They went inside, where the aroma of coffee mingled with the scent of cinnamon and nutmeg. Sam cleaned up at the kitchen sink, then joined everyone else at the table, where they made small talk while eating the best apple cobbler Simone had ever tasted.

Every once in a while, she caught one or the other of Mike's parents stealing a surreptitious glance her way.

Were they wondering if she and Mike were dating?

Did they know she was pregnant?

Before they'd come inside the house, Mike had insisted that he hadn't told them about the baby. Hopefully, he'd been truthful. It made her feel…uneasy to think Sam and Rhonda might be privy to the news, that they might sit in judgment over her decision to give up their grandchild.

But wouldn't it be worse to be a lousy mother?

Simone passed on the coffee, asking for water instead. And as they ate, Sam mentioned that Mike's sister Kathy had just been hired as a reporter for the *Walnut River Courier,* and that his younger brother Dave, was going to propose to the young woman he'd been dating since high school.

"Sammy has a Little League game on Saturday," Rhonda said. "He's going to play shortstop." She turned to Simone and explained, "Sammy is Aaron's son and our oldest grandchild."

"Are you going to the game?" Mike asked.

Sam beamed. "We wouldn't miss it."

"I'm even going to wear my lucky Baseball-Mama shirt." Rhonda turned to Simone. "I used to practically live down at the ball field when Mike and his brothers were young. And it's great to have a reason to go back and watch the kids play."

"I know it's only T-ball," Sam added, "but that boy is a natural-born athlete. And I'm not just saying that because he's my namesake."

"You ought to stop by on Saturday," Rhonda told Mike. "Sammy's game starts at noon."

"I've got to work," Mike said, "but I'll try to make the next one."

"And bring Simone with you," Sam said, a twinkle in his eye.

Simone didn't comment. She was both touched to have been included yet discomfited at the same time.

Before long, they'd finished their bowls of cobbler.

What was with all the conflicting emotions?

Simone found herself wanting to find an excuse to stay longer, but she wasn't any good at dealing with warm, fuzzy feelings. She always seemed to stiffen at the wrong time or say something that came across as awkward.

She did much better at the hospital, where she could just do the job she'd been trained to do. Where her efforts to provide comfort or understanding actually worked.

Fortunately, Mike stepped in and made it easy for her. "Simone and I have to go. I promised her we'd only stay a few minutes. Besides, I have a lot of work to do on that house."

"I can come over and help you rewire those electrical outlets," Sam said.

"Thanks, Dad." Mike gave his dad a hearty hug, then kissed his mom on the cheek.

It was nice to see the warmth the O'Rourkes showed each other.

Yet it also reminded Simone of all she'd missed growing up.

Chapter Eleven

Mike glanced across the vehicle to the passenger seat, where Simone sat, staring out the window at the passing scenery. "So, what did you think?"

She turned and caught his eye. "About what?"

"My parents."

"They're very nice. And you're lucky to have them."

The O'Rourkes could be her family, too, Mike thought. That is, if she was willing to accept them. But he decided it was best not to push her any more than he already had.

"What do you plan to do when you get back to your new house?" she asked.

Was she intentionally trying to change the subject?

Or did she just think it was time to move on to another topic?

Either way, he was okay with it—for now, anyway.

"Since I can't get the gas and electricity turned on until tomorrow afternoon, I figured it's a good idea to get those outlets changed. I also have a few light fixtures that need to be replaced. So I'm going to start with that."

"I guess that means you won't have lights or a television tonight."

He'd thought about that this morning, before he signed the lease and picked up the keys. But he had to work tomorrow and didn't want to put off moving in. He had a lot to do.

And a baby on the way.

"Most of my spare time will be spent on fix-it projects," he said, "so I won't be reading or watching much TV for a while."

"How long do you expect the project to take?"

Up until the baby was born, he suspected. "I'd like to have it done for the holidays, although I think the place will be an ongoing project."

"I'm glad it all worked out for you."

He probably would have bought that particular house anyway, even if Simone wasn't pregnant. Still, he was glad that things seemed to be coming together. "It's going to need new paint and window coverings, too, but I'd rather get the repair work done first. Of course, that's probably because I'm not that good at decorating. I never have had much of an eye for matching paint or fabric swatches."

"That's the fun part," Simone said.

That's what he'd been counting on. He slid another glance her way. "I don't suppose you'd mind helping me with that—would you?"

"Me?"

He didn't dare tell her the real reason he'd asked. That he hoped she'd live in the house with him someday. That he wanted her to leave her mark on their home, every wall, every room.

Instead, he told her, "You've done such a great job decorating your place, I thought you'd have some good suggestions for what I can do with mine."

"Thanks." She tucked a silky strand of hair behind her ear. "What did you want me to do?"

He didn't want it to seem like a big chore, so he shrugged. "Maybe you could come by later today or tomorrow and look around. I'm not all that fussy, but I would like the house to look nice inside. My folks always had off-white walls. But I've noticed some people get creative with colors these days. Not that I have time to look around when I'm called out on an emergency. But when it's a false alarm, I sometimes notice things like that."

"I guess it kind of depends upon what you like and the style of your furniture."

He laughed. "Other than a bedroom set, a state-of-the-art stereo system and a plasma television, I don't have furniture. In fact, I'll be eating out a lot because all the kitchen stuff belongs to Leif, and I had to leave it behind."

"That house is huge," she said. "So it's really going to look empty."

"I can always go to the thrift store and fill it up with things other people didn't want."

"Actually, because of the Victorian style, it might work to buy some antiques." She seemed to think on that for a while.

Before long, he pulled into Simone's driveway and parked. As they climbed from the Jeep, he spotted the dogs standing at the gate on the side of the house.

As Mike followed Simone up the walk, Woofer howled and Wags whined.

"Hey," Simone said to them. "Did you guys miss us?"

Miss *us?* He sure hoped she was starting to see them as a team.

He waited until she unlocked the door.

Once inside, she faced him, "Why don't you let the dogs in while I pack up a few things for Wags to take with him."

Moments later, while Mike stood in the living room, dividing his attention between the big and little dogs, Simone returned carrying a box.

"Thanks to Woofer, who seems to like the Puppy Bits much better than his own food, Wags is running low. He has enough to last him for a week or so, but you'll need to pick up some more the next time you go to the store."

"All right."

"And at night, I've been making him and Woofer stay in the kitchen, since he still tends to have an accident every now and then. But he's getting better." She scratched the puppy's ear. "Aren't you, little guy."

Mike couldn't help but notice that they'd been treating the two canines like children, that they'd both seemed to have taken on a parental role with the dogs.

Shouldn't Simone take that as a sign that she had a maternal streak after all and that she would love their baby?

That she wouldn't be a bad mother just because she'd been raised by one?

"You know, I was just thinking," he said. "Since I'll be working until it gets dark and I don't have anything in the kitchen to cook with, why don't I come back and take you out to dinner?"

"Won't you be tired?" she asked. "It sounds as though you have a lot to do."

He shrugged. "I still have to eat."

"Maybe it would be easier if I fixed dinner for you."

Mike shot her a crooked grin as he realized his game plan was moving along just fine. "I'd like that. Thanks for the invitation."

"What time will you be ready to eat?"

"You tell me."

"How about six?"

"Perfect. I'll see you then."

As Mike carried Wags out to the Jeep, he couldn't help but feel relieved.

Everything was coming together nicely.

After finishing the laundry and cleaning the bathrooms, Simone took a shower and shampooed her hair. She used a fluffy, white towel to dry off. As she bent to get her feet, a bout of dizziness struck.

Ooh. She carefully straightened and reached for the countertop to steady herself.

That didn't happen very often.

She'd gotten dizzy once before, though, and had fainted at the pet shop. Dr. Kipper had said it sometimes happened during pregnancy and had suggested she eat regularly and change positions slowly.

Should she mention it to the doctor again? Just to be sure?

She had more than herself to worry about these days.

Once she'd dressed, styled her hair and put on a dab of lipstick and mascara, she drove to the New England Ranch Market. Surprisingly, she got a spot right in front, which didn't happen often. The popular grocery store was pretty busy in the afternoons.

She snatched her purse from the passenger seat, slipping the strap over her shoulder, then locked the car and went inside.

A display of fresh flowers sat at the doorway, tempting her to buy an unadvertised special—tulips.

Why not?

She grabbed a yellow bouquet, placed them in her shopping cart and headed for the produce section, where she picked up potatoes, carrots, celery and several bags of fresh fruit. Next she went to the butcher shop, where she chose a small rump roast to make for dinner.

Should she make dessert or buy it?

While she was trying to decide, a male voice called out her name. "Simone! Fancy meeting you here."

She turned to see Fred Baxter, his cart filled to the brim. She greeted the man and asked about Millie. "I suppose she's holding down the fort at Tails a Waggin'."

"Actually, she picked up a flu bug and is home sick again today."

"That's too bad." Simone didn't like to see anyone feeling under the weather.

"Yes, it is. Poor thing. I worked part of the day, then closed the shop early." He scratched his head. "Do you know where I can find the chicken soup? Millie said they make a homemade variety in the back that doesn't have all the preservatives and stuff, and she thought that might help her feel better."

Besides its quality meat and produce, the New England Ranch Market also offered an assortment of home-style meals that could be purchased for those on the go.

Simone pointed to the east wall. "You'll find it in the refrigerator section."

"Thanks. The shopping is usually Millie's job, so I'm not familiar with the layout here."

For a guy who didn't know his way around a market, Fred had sure managed to find plenty of things to buy. She glanced into his cart, noting the sugary brand of cereal that kids liked, two gallon jugs of milk, individual packets of raisins, peanut butter, jelly, those little fruit juices that came in a ten-pack, Popsicles…

Somehow, she expected he'd be picking up more adult food, like steaks, potatoes, maybe even a six-pack of beer…

"What's the matter?" Fred asked.

"Oh, I…" She shrugged. "I don't know. I just noticed that you're buying a lot of things that children would like—which is fine. It surprised me a bit. That's all."

Fred chuckled. "Yes, I did my best to choose things that would appeal to kids. We got a call from the pastor of our church last night regarding some children that needed a temporary home."

"And you and Millie are going to take them?" Simone asked.

"It's only for a week, I guess. And even though Millie hasn't been able to keep much of anything down for the past few days, she insisted that they stay with us. Can you believe it?" Fred slowly shook his head. "I told her the timing was bad, and that maybe it would be better if someone else volunteered their home, but Millie…" Fred chuckled and gave a little shrug. "Well, you know Millie. She has a heart for kids."

That was so true. All Simone had to do was to offer her baby to the Baxters, and she knew Millie would be thrilled. But a sense of uneasiness settled over her, leaving her with second thoughts about giving up the baby.

Yet she was a realist.

She had to be.

It wasn't as if Simone didn't care about the baby. It was because she wanted to do the right thing. And it was obvious that Millie would make a much better mother.

"Well," Fred said, nodding toward the east wall. "I'd better go get that soup."

"I sure hope Millie kicks that virus soon," Simone said, "especially if she's going to have to babysit."

"Me, too."

"Be sure to tell her hello for me."

"I will." Fred began to push his cart down the aisle, then tossed her a grin. "Have a nice evening."

"Thanks. You, too." Simone glanced down at the pot roast and the yellow tulips.

Interestingly enough, she *did* expect to have a nice evening.

Mike arrived at Simone's house about a minute or two before six o'clock.

He hoped she didn't mind him bringing Wags along, too. The poor little guy started whining up a storm when Mike tried to stick him behind the gate he'd stretched across the kitchen doorway. And he hadn't had the heart to leave him all by himself.

So with Wags cuddled in the crook of one arm, he used his free hand to ring the bell. He didn't have to wait very long for Simone to answer.

She wore a red apron over a pair of brown slacks and a cream-colored blouse. Her hair was down and curled at the shoulders—just the way he liked it.

He couldn't help thinking how great it would be to come home to her and the baby each night. According to his calculations, she was due around Thanksgiving.

As the middle child in a family of five kids, Mike's best memories were of holidays, campouts and outdoor games with his siblings. So he looked forward to seeing his son or daughter joining his or her cousins during the O'Rourke-family functions.

"Well, look who else came to dinner," Simone said.

"I…uh…" He glanced at the wiggly pup. "I hated to leave with him crying. I hope you don't mind that I brought him."

Her smile, which dimpled her cheeks and put a sparkle in her eyes, just about knocked the breath right out of him. "I would have been upset if you'd left him home alone in a dark house."

That was good to know. Wags had wormed his way into Simone's heart, just the way the baby would.

Simone gripped Woofer by his collar and held him at bay as Mike entered and caught the aroma of something warm and meaty—beef?—that permeated the air. He'd gone without lunch today and was starving, so he inhaled deeply and relished the hearty, mouth-watering smell.

Once the door shut behind him, he placed Wags on the floor so the two canine buddies could play.

"How was your day?" Simone asked as she led him to the small dining area that was an extension of the living room.

"It was great. My dad brought my brother Nick, and between the three of us, we changed out the plumbing and light fixtures before I had to be at work. So it was a good start." He watched the back of her as she walked, watched the gentle sway of her hips.

Yep. He could sure see himself coming home to Simone.

"I hope you had a good day, too," he said.

"Actually, I did. I ran some errands, cleaned out the fridge and fixed dinner—speaking of which, I hope you like pot roast."

"I sure do. And if it tastes as good as it smells, you probably won't have any leftovers to worry about."

She blessed him with a shy smile. "I don't usually cook for anyone, so it was…fun." She shrugged, a pair of pretty dimples forming.

Good. That was another indication that she might be warming up to the idea of home and hearth and family.

He noticed that she'd set the table, complete with linen napkins. The centerpiece was a white vase of yellow tulips. "That's a nice touch. The guys down at the department all take turns with the meal preparation, but none of them put flowers out."

She smiled. "I don't usually get fancy, but they were on sale at the market today, and I love tulips."

He made a mental note of that.

"If you'll take a seat," she said, "I'll bring out the food."

"Is there something I can do to help?"

"No, I've got it under control. But what can I bring you to drink?"

"Whatever you're having is fine."

"Milk?"

For the baby? Probably, which was another sign that she was slowly shifting into maternal mode.

Mike didn't drink much milk these days, but he would be supportive of her efforts to be healthy for the baby's sake. "Sure. Milk sounds good to me."

Minutes later, they sat across the table from each other. The pot roast, carrots, potatoes and gravy looked even better than they smelled, and it seemed as though he'd been invited to dine with the queen.

Of course, he suspected they could have been munching on bologna sandwiches and corn chips, and he would have felt the same way.

They talked about life in the E.R., as well as the fire department. Mike told her about some of the practical jokes he and Leif had pulled on their buddies, which she seemed to appreciate. So he went on to reveal a side of his friend and partner she hadn't been aware of.

"Mo Granger has this habit of sleeping with his arm under his pillow at night," Mike said, "so once, after having spaghetti for dinner, Leif, who had kitchen duty, snuck the table scraps into the bedroom, lifted the pillow from Mo's bed, and dumped a pile of noodles and sauce right on the mattress. Then he carefully replaced the pillow."

"Ooh." Simone scrunched her face, yet the hint of a smile remained. "That's gross."

"Yep. And you should have seen what happened when Mo climbed into bed that night and tried to get comfortable. His hand slipped under his pillow and right into a slimy mess. Mo was hopping mad, while the rest of us laughed our heads off."

"I can't imagine Leif doing something like that."

Mike laughed. "Apparently, he learned that trick on a Boy Scout campout, and now it's become sort of an initiation we do with each new rookie. We welcome them with a spaghetti dinner, making sure there's more than enough for everyone, then Leif hides the leftovers in their beds."

"That's terrible." A grin suggested she found it funny, too. "Those poor rookies."

"Hey, but what goes around comes around. Once, when some of us were off duty, we met at the Brown Jug, that bar located just off Lexington and Riverdale. After a while, Leif excused himself to go to the restroom. And when he came back, he'd forgotten to zip his fly."

Simone arched a brow, while a smile tugged at her lips.

"Wally Wainwright, one of the rookies who'd had the pleasure of Leif's leftover-pasta humor, spotted it first and offered him twenty bucks to stand on the table and tell a joke while facing a table of very attractive and obviously single ladies."

"Uh-oh." Simone leaned forward and placed her elbows on the table. "Then what happened?"

"Leif had a little liquid courage in his system, especially since I was the designated driver that night, so he took the bet and climbed on the table. Trouble was, he was flashing a pair of tightie-whities and didn't realize it.

"One of the ladies noticed, and they started nudging each other. The next thing you know, they all busted up laughing."

"That must have been a sight."

"'*Hey*,' Leif said to the women. 'Why are you laughing? I didn't even get to the punch line yet.'" Mike couldn't help chuckling himself.

"I had no idea Leif was a practical jokester," Simone said.

"Well, he is. But this time the joke was on him."

"I guess it was." Simone had fallen into an easy mood. It was great to hear her laugh. And sitting across from her, with the candlelight dancing upon the gold highlights in her hair and her eyes sparkling with humor, was a real treat.

He wished that she could see herself like this—the Simone he'd fallen in love with.

"By the way," Mike added, "Leif loves to sing, although he's not as talented as he'd like to think he is. So if you're into karaoke, we'll have to invite him to go with us."

"I'm afraid I'm not at all comfortable standing before a crowd, let alone entertaining one. But it would be fun to go out with Leif sometime."

"I'll see what I can arrange." A double date might be nice.

After dinner and a bowl of rocky road for dessert, Simone stood and began to clear the table.

Mike followed suit.

"You don't have to help," she said. "I can clean up after you leave."

"I can't let you do that. My mom would skin me alive if I left you with the mess. Besides, it's quick work when two people share the load."

And it was. Before long, they had the leftovers packed away and the dining room back in order.

Mike had just filled the dishwasher when Simone turned away from wiping down the stove, the dishcloth in her hand. She'd no more than started to walk back to the sink when Woofer came charging into the room with Wags at his heels.

The big dog's hind end, which had a tendency to sway to one side while his front end was going another, thumped into Simone and knocked her off balance.

Mike had always been quick on his feet, but the thought of her taking a tumble in her condition sent a jolt of adrenaline to jump-start his natural reaction.

"Are you all right?" he asked as he caught her in his arms.

"Yes, but darn that crazy dog…" She looked up at him, and their gazes met. Locked.

Something passed between them, something blood-stirring and heart-pounding. Something that set off the pheromones and hormones that always seemed to be buzzing and sparking between them like a swarm of fireflies.

Mike was doing his best to shrug it off, to keep his mind off what he'd been wanting to do again since the last time he'd kissed her.

But when Simone reached up and stroked his cheek, when her lips parted…

Well, damn. He was only human.

Chapter Twelve

As Mike took her in his arms and lowered his mouth to hers, Simone had only a moment to question whether she wanted to kiss him again.

But something had happened to her tonight. Something that hadn't been triggered or altered by a champagne buzz. And she wondered if maybe Mike could be right about her.

About *them*.

She certainly couldn't deny how badly she wanted to kiss him, how badly her body yearned for what only Mike could give her.

As his lips brushed across hers, as she allowed his tongue to sweep inside her mouth, she lost all conscious thought.

The only thing left for her to do was to hold on tight

and ride the wave of passion that swept through her, hoping that somehow she could get her fill of him.

As the kiss deepened, raw need took over. Hands explored, stroked, caressed, while breaths mingled and heat exploded in a sexual rush.

Simone hadn't wanted to get physically involved with Mike again, but she'd grown to care for him—more than she'd wanted to admit. And at this very moment, she knew she'd be a fool not to admit it or do something about it.

So she broke the kiss long enough to rest her cheek against his, to catch her breath and whisper, "There's no arguing that we have chemistry."

"That's for sure." His embrace loosened, yet he didn't let go.

She clung to him, too, savoring the musky male scent of his mountain-fresh aftershave for a moment longer. Then she slowly pulled away and raked a hand through the strands of her hair. "I still have reservations about us getting further involved, but I want you. And I want to make love again."

"I'm glad." Desire smoldered in his eyes as he moved slowly, deliberately, closing the gap between them.

He cupped her cheeks with his hands, and his thumbs caressed her skin, as the intensity of his gaze weakened her knees.

"You won't be sorry about this, Simone." The sincerity in his passion-laced tone reached deep into her heart, and she hoped he was right.

She might have reservations about making love with a man who wanted so much more than she was able to give him, but no one had ever made her feel so special, so desired. So…flawless.

What little apprehension she'd had left seemed to vanish within the sexually charged room, and she slipped her arms around his neck and pulled him back into another heated kiss.

Their tongues dipped and tasted, and she was lost in a mind-spinning swirl of heat and desire.

His hands slid possessively up and down her back, then he gripped her derriere and pulled her flush against his erection, staking his claim and letting her know that he wanted her as badly as she wanted him.

As his hands slipped under her blouse, his fingertips skimmed her skin, and her breath caught. She'd never been so fully aroused, and she had a sudden compulsion to shed her clothing, to remove all the physical barriers that kept her from enjoying him freely.

She tore her mouth away from his long enough to reach for the hem of her blouse and to say, "Wait a minute. Let me get this…"

He took the lead, helping her to slide the fabric over her head and to unhook her white, satiny bra. Before she knew it, she was tugging his shirt out of his pants and grappling for his belt at the same time.

Apparently, he was glad to assist, because he'd soon bared his torso, too.

Simone wanted Mike, wanted *this*. And nothing else seemed to matter. As she fell into his embrace, she relished the feel of her breasts as they pressed against his chest, the beat of her heart as it pounded against his.

But it wasn't nearly enough.

As he nuzzled the soft spot below her ear and trailed kisses along her neck, he whispered between ragged breaths, "I want to touch and kiss you all over."

He wouldn't get an argument from her. "Okay, but I don't think my knees are going to hold me up much longer."

"No problem." He scooped her into his arms, then carried her to the bed, where he gently laid her down and proceeded to peel her slacks over her hips. Next he took off her panties, leaving her completely naked.

"Now, you," she said, feeling like a seductress with her hair splayed upon the pillow sham. "I'm not the only one who's going to get kissed all over."

All over, huh?

Mike grinned. "Honey, I'm going to hold you to it." He peeled off his own pants and dropped them on the floor, then he joined her on the bed, where he loved her with his hands, with his mouth—slowly and methodically, as he savored each sensual touch, each breathy kiss, each flick of the tongue.

And he didn't let up the sensual assault until he'd made her writhe with need.

"I want you inside of me," she said, her voice ragged with desire. "All of you."

"You can have every last inch." Of course, he'd already given her more than that. She had him—heart and soul—but he didn't dare admit it. Nor did he mention that he'd been dreaming of doing this again since the end of February, when they'd made love the first time.

As he hovered over her, he inhaled the powdery, peach fragrance of her body lotion, as well as the musky scent of sex. And when she opened for him, he entered full hilt.

She arched to meet each thrust, in and out, until they peaked, until they pressed over the top and cried out in a mind-shattering, body-shuddering climax.

They continued to hold each other, as though neither wanted to be the first to move, the first to break the tenuous connection that stretched between them.

As the last wave of pleasure passed, Mike rolled to the side, taking her with him.

He expected her to pull away, to shut down like she had the last time. But she held on tight, her nails threatening to make crescent-shaped marks on his back.

It had been a sweet joining, one that he hoped meant she'd finally accepted his love and all he had to offer her and their baby.

It's what he'd been counting on—that she would finally be able to let go of the past and embrace the future.

A future with him.

As dawn cast its light in the bedroom, Simone lay cuddled in Mike's arms, her back to his front, her bare bottom nestled in the fold of his lap.

They'd made love several times last night, with each climax better than the last. So they'd found themselves in a sensual world of their own, oblivious to anything but each other.

The phone had rung around nine o'clock, but Simone had let the answering machine pick up. Nothing seemed to matter except pleasuring each other.

They hadn't even bothered to gate the kitchen, which meant the dogs had remained loose in the house last night, so she'd probably find a puddle or two on the floor.

Around midnight, since Mike had to go into the station in the morning, he got out of bed long enough to set the alarm.

Otherwise, they'd savored every moment together.

The very first time they'd made love, that night in February, Simone had awakened with a growing sense of regret.

She felt better about it today, though, and didn't have that same compulsion to retreat. Still, she was on edge.

Would she gradually get used to waking in Mike's arms? To having him in her life?

He seemed to think she would.

Woofer, who'd just trotted into the bedroom, placed his nose on the mattress and whimpered, letting her know he wanted to go into the backyard. So she carefully lifted Mike's arm and slid out of his embrace. Then she climbed from bed and pulled her bathrobe from the closet.

As her bare feet padded across the hardwood floor, the dogs eagerly followed her through the kitchen and to the service porch, where she opened the back door and let them outside.

Wags hardly made it to the lawn before squatting to relieve himself.

Hey. Maybe she wouldn't find any puddles on the floor after all.

"Good job, Wags! That's the idea." She pulled the lapel of her robe closer, shielding her naked body from the brisk morning air and wishing she'd taken time to put on her slippers.

She decided to leave the dogs outdoors to play for a while, then went inside and put on a small pot of coffee for Mike. In the meantime, the alarm sounded in the bedroom, then shut off. A moment later, the plumbing shuddered as the shower went on.

Mike would be leaving soon, so they'd have to discuss the future later, which was okay with her. She wasn't sure what she wanted out of a relationship with him anyway.

Whenever she thought about marriage, she still grew uneasy. And unfortunately, the white-picket-fence dream was still Mike's highest priority and Simone's biggest fear.

And why shouldn't it be?

No matter what Mike said, what he might think, Simone knew she would fall sadly short of the wife-and-mother image he had in mind. She'd never be like Rhonda O'Rourke, and Mike would end up disappointed down the road. And that wasn't fair to him.

Bottom line? Simone was a career woman, a medical professional who loved doing what she'd been trained to do.

Would Mike expect her to be a stay-at-home mother?

She certainly hoped not. That would be a huge conflict in and of itself. How could she give up the one thing that defined her?

She couldn't.

Would that make her a bad mother? Would Mike grow to resent her because of it? And worse—would the baby?

As the last bit of water trickled through the filter and filled the bottom half of the carafe with fresh coffee, she glanced at the answering machine that rested on the counter. A red light blinked to remind her of the call she hadn't wanted to take last night. So she pushed play, then listened for the message.

"Hi, Simone. It's Cynthia Pryor again. You know, your mom's friend and neighbor? I really hate to bother you, but I was wondering if—since you're a nurse—you could give me the name of a good counselor. I think your mother really needs to talk to someone, and…well, I'm out of my league when it comes to…some of her issues."

Had Simone's mom finally leveled with someone about the date rape?

If Simone hadn't found those journals, she might never have known why her mother couldn't stand looking at her.

"I hate to pry," Cynthia began, "but when I told Susan to call you, she admitted that your relationship wasn't very good, and that it was probably her fault."

Probably?

"Gosh," Cynthia said. "Here I am, rambling on your tape. You probably think I'm a mindless old busybody…"

Actually, the thought had crossed Simone's mind, although Simone suspected she meant well.

"But it breaks my heart to see the sadness in your mother's eyes, especially when I think there's relief out there—either with medication or by talking it out. So, anyway, would you please give me—or better yet, give *her* a call? Your mother really needs someone in her corner right now."

Cynthia went on to leave her number before hanging up.

Susan Garner *did* need help, and Simone couldn't help wondering where someone like Cynthia had been years ago. Back when Simone had needed someone in her corner. Back when Simone *also* needed a mommy.

So why should she get involved *now?*

The last time Cynthia had encouraged Simone to pick up the phone and offer some daughterly advice, it had taken her mother more than a week to return the call.

No, if her mom had wanted Simone to get involved, Cynthia wouldn't have had to interfere. Her mother would have picked up the phone and called herself.

Really? a small voice asked. *Considering how lousy your relationship has been?*

"That's *not* my fault," Simone muttered.

She opened the fridge, removed a carton of orange juice and poured herself a glass. Then she divided an English muffin and placed both sides in the toaster. She'd intended to fix Mike a hearty breakfast this morning, but the message from Cynthia seemed to have depleted her domestic energy.

"Good morning." Mike entered the kitchen wearing a towel wrapped around his waist and a carefree grin. His hair was wet and mussed, his body still damp from the shower.

She returned his smile, hoping it hadn't fallen short of sincere.

He bent to kiss her, and she offered her cheek.

Darn it. It was happening again. He was coming on strong, and she was pulling back.

She wished she could make an excuse for doing so. Or maybe find a way to regroup. But thoughts of her mother and old childhood pain had set her on autopilot.

Mike didn't seem to have let the proffered cheek bother him. "I'd like to take you to dinner as soon as we're both free. How does your schedule look?"

"I'm off tonight and work tomorrow." Actually, she was glad they would both be tied up for a few days. She was starting to gravitate toward him, yet old habits were hard to kick.

He closed the gap between them, and she forced her feet to stay still, her smile to remain in place.

See? She didn't have to retreat. She could make a conscious effort to remain emotionally connected.

He placed a hand along the side of her head, caressed the strands of her hair. Then he snagged her gaze with his. "Last night was wonderful for me. And it was great for you, too. You can't deny that."

"You're right."

"Why do I sense that you're having second thoughts?"

She couldn't see any point mentioning that her mother was still casting a dark shadow over her life. That there was still a little girl inside of Simone who hoped her mommy would get help, that she'd learn how to love the child she'd given birth to. "I guess it's just because I've gotten so used to living alone that I'm not sure what we're supposed to do now."

"Well, that's an easy decision this morning. I'm going to have a cup of coffee, get dressed and leave you to spend your day and evening any way you want." He placed a finger under her chin. "Then I'm going to work, where I'll probably think about you too damn much."

"The whole commitment thing scares me, Mike."

"I know it does, honey."

God, what did she do to deserve a guy like him loving her? He was so understanding. And she was so…

She blew out a ragged sigh. "I just need some time to get used to…this."

"Get used to what? *Me? Us?*"

She nodded. "I was raised differently than you. I'm not used to the home-and-hearth stuff. Heck, I don't even read romances or watch chick flicks. It's hard for me to relate to the characters."

"Fred and Millie are happily married. Are you uncomfortable around them?"

"No. Not at all."

"What about my folks? You seemed to enjoy yourself at their house."

"I did." Still, as nice as the O'Rourkes were, as accepting as they'd been, Simone had only been further convinced of the differences she and Mike had.

Rhonda O'Rourke might be the epitome of a loving mom and grandma, but being around her only made Simone realize how much she'd missed growing up.

"Then don't fight it, Simone. Just give it a chance, honey. You'll get used to me, to us. You'll see."

The English muffin popped up in the toaster, and she turned to get it, retreating from the intensity of his gaze, from the emotion of the topic.

"Maybe you ought to start reading more romances and watching more movies. It might help."

But before she could take a plate out of the cupboard to put the muffin halves on, she thought of something. Something she'd been wondering about.

She turned to face him again. "Why did you take me to your parents' house yesterday?"

"Because I wanted you to meet my mom and dad, to see what kind of grandparents they'll be."

"I have no doubt that they'll be wonderful," she admitted. "It's just that I still can't see myself making you happy in the long run."

"Let me be the judge of that."

"Making a marriage work is tough enough when people come from the same background," she said.

"Marriages are two parts love, one part compromise. That's something my parents always told me."

She supposed that was true. "It's hard to imagine them having to compromise about anything."

"Over the years, there were plenty of times. For one thing, my dad was raised Catholic, and my mom was Protestant. But they didn't let that stop them. They loved each other and were determined to make their marriage work."

Still, she couldn't help thinking that there'd be way too much compromising going on if Mike had his way. And she couldn't help thinking she'd be doing them all a favor by avoiding what would only be a star-crossed affair.

But truthfully, there was a part of her that really wanted to adopt Mike's optimism, his unshakable belief that everything would work out. That she would instantly fall in love with the baby the moment she laid eyes on it. That Susan Garner hadn't left any permanent scars on Simone's psyche, other than to make her grow up afraid to love, afraid to get involved with the nicest guy in the world.

A man any other woman would be thrilled to call her own.

A man who'd helped her touch the moon and stars last night.

"I guess I just need time to get used to this, Mike."

"No problem. You've got it." Then he brushed a kiss upon her cheek. "I'm going to get dressed, then get out of your hair for a few days."

That ought to be a big relief.

So why wasn't it?

* * *

Mike should have been walking on air after spending last night in Simone's bed and in her arms. In fact, up until six this morning, he'd thought he *had* been.

But Simone had done it to him again. She'd ditched the warm, loving woman she'd been at bedtime and morphed into someone he couldn't seem to get through to. A woman so reserved that she might shatter in his arms.

At the station, his shift had barely started when the crew was called out to rescue a child in a tree. It had been one of those so-called emergencies that was actually humorous.

Tommy the cat, a big orange tabby, had gotten stuck in a tree. And when little Jimmy Ralston took it upon himself to rescue the frightened feline, Tommy had scampered down, leaving the ten-year-old boy about twenty feet aboveground and afraid to move.

Twenty minutes later, they'd put the boy on the ground and placed him in the custody of his mother. They'd just started back to the station when another call came in. This time, it was a kitchen fire started by a woman who hadn't had a match to light her fireplace. Instead, she'd used a twisted-up paper towel that she lit at the stove. She'd started to carry it like a small torch into the living room, but the paper burned much faster than she'd intended.

The panicked woman rushed to the sink, only to watch the flame catch the curtains on fire.

Fortunately, no one had been hurt.

Now, as noon approached, Mike found himself sitting all by himself on the side of his bed, his mind on Simone and their problems. She was pushing him to the limit of his patience. He'd told her he would give her all the time she needed, but now he wasn't so sure he could do that.

Not if she refused to meet him at least part of the way.

"O'Rourke," Leif said as he approached. "What's wrong?"

"Nothing." What was he supposed to say? That he was bummed out because Simone was pulling away again?

Leif had already suggested he cut bait and run, so he knew what advice his buddy would give him this time.

Of course, things weren't quite as bad as they'd been at the end of February. And maybe she would realize that she'd still have plenty of space and alone time.

"What's eating you?" Leif asked.

Nothing Mike felt like sharing. "I'm just sorting through a few things. No big deal."

"Is Simone giving you fits again?"

Mike wanted to say yes, to lay his heart on the line. But somehow, it didn't feel right going into detail about the woman he loved, about their relationship—what there was of one, anyway.

"No. It's not that," he lied. "Don't worry about me. I'll be okay."

And he would be—one way or another.

Leif chuffed, then took a seat across the table. "I think you just need to get laid. That ought to put things into perspective for you."

Oh, yeah? He *had* gotten laid. And it seemed to have made things worse.

"Come on," Mike said, getting to his feet and trying his best to pull himself out of a bum mood. "Let's go watch ESPN. There's a game on."

Still, it was going to be tough keeping his mind on anything other than Simone.

Especially when she was frustrating the hell out of him, and he wasn't sure how much longer he could deal with her refusal to give their love—or their family—a chance.

What if she never would?

Chapter Thirteen

On Sunday afternoon, before starting her shift, Simone stopped by the solarium, where Henry Weisfield's party was being held. She really didn't feel like celebrating— or mixing—but she managed to put on a happy face, determined to make a showing and to wish the retiring hospital administrator her best.

Upon entering the festively decorated room, Simone surveyed her surroundings, as well as those who'd stopped to congratulate Henry.

She spotted Ella and J.D. mingling in the crowd, so she made her way to the happy couple to say hello and to congratulate J.D. on his new position, which he would assume Monday morning. By the time J.D. entered the hospital for his first day on the job, Henry and his wife would be flying over the Atlantic on their

way to Europe, where they would set sail on a Mediter-
ranean cruise they'd been planning for months.

After Simone chatted with J.D. and Ella for a few
minutes, she excused herself to speak to Henry. Even
though he'd recently been sympathetic toward an NHC
takeover, she still appreciated his years of service.

"Enjoy your retirement," she told the older man.
"And have a wonderful time on that cruise."

"Thank you, Simone. My wife and I are eager to do
a lot of traveling." Henry shook her hand and grinned,
then turned to the next person who'd approached to
greet him and wish him well.

With the formalities out of the way, Simone stopped
by the refreshment table and, using the ladle provided,
filled a large glass of punch.

"I hope you're going to save some for me."

She turned to see Isobel standing behind her and
smiled. "That shouldn't be a problem. Everyone else
seems to be having wine or champagne."

While in front of the bowl, she prepared a glass for
the hospital social worker.

Isobel didn't usually work on Sundays, so Simone
was glad to see that she'd come. It would give her an
opportunity to get the referral for a counselor.

"You're wearing scrubs," Isobel said, "so you're obviously working today."

"My shift starts in a few minutes, so I can't stay long,
but I wanted to give Henry my best." Simone scanned the
room, making sure she could speak in confidence, then
lowered her voice. "I must admit, though, it's probably
in the hospital's best interests that he's retiring."

Henry's empathy toward an NHC takeover had contributed to some of the dissension on the board.

"J.D. ought to be a good replacement," Isobel said, glancing around the room, as well, apparently satisfied that their conversation would be private. "By the way, I have a growing suspicion about the person who is leaking information about the hospital to NHC."

"What's that?"

"I think the mole is in one of the administrative departments."

That was unsettling, but certainly possible. "Do you think Henry is—or rather *was*—the mole?"

"I didn't mean to imply *that*. But it's obvious someone in that department has been talking out of turn."

They each took a sip of punch and watched the people who'd gathered in the solarium—those in street clothes who weren't working and those in lab jackets and scrubs who were.

"You know," Simone said, "I want to ask you something. My mom needs to see a counselor. She never sought any professional help after that date rape I told you about. Is there anyone you can recommend? She'd also do well in some kind of support group."

"If you'll walk with me to my office, I'll give you some names and contact numbers."

Simone agreed, and they left the solarium together.

"I've pretty much given up hope that I'll ever have a close relationship with my mother," Simone said, "but either way, she still needs to come to grips with what happened to her."

"Talking it out helps a lot of people."

Simone walked along in silence for a while, then

said, "Sometimes I think I might need to talk to someone, too."

"You'd be surprised at what an hour or two with a trained counselor can do."

"I'll give it some thought." Simone blew out a sigh. "You know, I've always had intimacy problems, so I tend to keep to myself. I was doing just fine until Mike came into the picture."

"That's understandable."

Was it? She hoped so. And she couldn't help adding, "I'm having trouble trusting him to love the real me."

"Sometimes, trust is a decision that's made."

"Like blind faith?"

"No. Not like that. Trust is earned, but there are times when you must cognitively decide to trust someone."

"And what if that person lets you down? Or, in this case, what if I disappoint Mike?"

"That's the risk we take in any relationship."

Simone offered her friend a wistful smile. "I'm not much of an emotional risk-taker."

"Then I suppose you have to ask yourself if you love each other enough to handle life's normal disappointments."

"That's the problem. I don't know what I feel for him. I think it's love. And if so, I'm not sure what my love— or *his*—can handle."

Isobel placed a hand on Simone's shoulder. "You can't change the past, but you can change your perception of it."

Maybe so. But as usual, she just couldn't seem to forget about the kind of mother she'd had. The kind of mother she was so afraid she would become.

"Families are created by love," Isobel said, "not necessarily by blood."

"I know. You're right." That's why Simone had hoped Millie and Fred could create that kind of special, loving family for her baby.

"I'd be happy to talk to you—as a friend," Isobel said. "Or I can refer you to a counselor, if you think that might be more helpful. A couple of sessions might be all it will take."

"You mean you don't see me needing extensive therapy?"

"In your case, I suspect the answer is already in your mind and in your heart. You probably just need someone to ask the right questions so you can sort through things and come up with your own conclusion, your own game plan."

Isobel opened her office door, then flipped through her Rolodex and jotted down a few names and numbers. "Give these to your mother. And if you decide you'd like a reference for yourself, let me know."

"All right. Thanks."

After Isobel locked up her office, the two women walked down the hall together. At the elevator, they went their separate ways—Isobel back to the party and Simone to work.

On the way to the E.R., she slipped her hand into her pocket, where she'd tucked the referrals, then made a detour to the hospital gardens, where she found some solitude.

She took a seat on one of the benches and pulled out her cell phone. She'd planned to call information to get Cynthia's number, but her movements froze.

Instead, she listened to her heart and dialed her mother's house. They'd been tiptoeing around an emotional quagmire for years, and Simone simply wasn't going to do it anymore.

When Susan Garner answered, Simone decided to be honest for the first time in her life. "Mom, it's me. I think you should get some counseling, and I have the names and contact info for some qualified therapists you might find helpful."

"I…well…actually, I've been thinking about it lately."

Good. They were on the right track, and she felt her heart swell with something she couldn't quite identify. Relief? Optimism?

"I'm glad to hear it." So she recited the names Isobel had given her, waiting as her mother made a note of them.

"Thanks," her mom said. "I may give someone a call. We'll see."

Simone decided to go one step further, again making the cognitive decision to trust herself and her instincts. "I never mentioned this to you before, but I know the circumstances surrounding my conception, Mom. And, well, I don't believe you've ever worked through your pain, which has crippled you in many ways. But I want you to know that I love you. And I'll be there for you…if you want me to."

For a long, drawn-out minute, the only response was silence.

Then came a gulp. "Oh, Simone…"

And the call ended in tears.

By the time Tuesday rolled around, Simone found herself restless and uneasy.

She also had a growing compulsion to talk to Mike. In fact, she couldn't get him out of her mind. He'd been on duty Saturday, and she'd had to work on Sunday, so she understood why they hadn't had any contact. In the past, she would have been happy to have the space, but for some reason she wasn't.

Then, late Monday morning, he'd called to say hello, but went on to tell her he had a full day scheduled at his new place.

That, too, was a reasonable excuse.

Still, she sensed a growing distance between them, which was unsettling.

She couldn't help wishing something would bring him to the E.R. Not that she wanted to wish bad health or injury on anyone. In the past, he'd managed to stop by a time or two, even without a patient. So it seemed like a reasonable wish on her part.

Throughout the day, she'd had a growing compulsion to pick up the phone and call his cell, yet she hadn't.

What would she have said? "I just wanted to hear your voice?"

It was true, though; she was definitely missing him.

But if she told him so, she wasn't sure if she was ready for what the truth might provoke.

So now Simone was in the midst of a day shift she was covering for Carol Harrington, an RN who'd sprained her ankle while playing with her granddaughter at the park.

As footsteps sounded and someone approached the nurses' desk, Simone glanced up from her work and saw Owen Randall, the new chief of staff.

Dr. Randall wore a pair of black slacks, a white shirt

and a lime-green-and-pink tie that would have been too bold for most men, but Owen was able to pull it off. "I thought I'd spread the word. Neil Kane, the insurance investigator from the state attorney general's office, arrived today and has begun a preliminary investigation of those allegations of insurance fraud."

Simone's stomach lurched. She knew the claims of fraud at Walnut River General made the possibility of a takeover more likely, so now that the investigation had begun, it all seemed real.

And threatening.

"Obviously, I'm not the least bit happy about Kane being here," Owen said, "but there's nothing I can do about it. Hopefully, he'll come to a quick conclusion about the integrity of the hospital, especially in regard to insurance billings."

"Have you met him yet?"

"Yes. Earlier this morning. I'm sure he'll eventually get around to interviewing you, so I wanted to give you a heads-up."

Great.

As Dr. Randall turned to go, Jennifer Dimon, one of the LVNs, approached the desk and called her name.

"Yes?" Simone answered.

"We've got a three-year-old little girl in bed five, and both parents are with her. She has an arm injury, and while I was getting her vitals, she claimed that 'Mommy did it.'"

Simone stiffened. She'd seen her share of child-abuse cases, and they never got easier. "I'd better talk to them."

Jennifer nodded. "Should I call Isobel?"

"Yes, we need to follow protocol." Simone stood. "I'll go back into the exam area with you."

Once behind the curtain, Simone introduced herself to the parents.

"It was an accident," the mother said, tears welling in her eyes. "I was trying to hold her hand, and she threw a fit. I didn't mean to jerk up as she was pulling away, and…"

The father slipped his arm around his wife's shoulder. "Lisa is a strong-willed little girl. And sometimes, she does that when walking with me. She'll just decide she doesn't want to go and lift up her legs."

"Those things happen," Simone said, still not sure if the mother had been abusive or whether it had been a routine accident.

They'd seen similar injuries before, when a child's shoulder or elbow was dislocated. But there were other situations in which the arm was twisted or jerked in an unnatural direction—the result of parental anger and abuse.

The pediatrician would have to make that call.

Still, her heart went out to the little girl, and she hoped this was merely the accident the parents claimed it was.

Simone couldn't help thinking back on the times when she'd been spanked or slapped for no apparent reason, times she'd cried herself to sleep, thinking she was a bad girl and trying to figure out what she'd done wrong.

Looking back now, though, she realized that her mother sometimes drank in the evenings, most likely as a way to cope with her own terrible demons. And that she probably hadn't been sober on those occasions that she'd lashed out at Simone.

But that hadn't made her actions less abusive.

Nor did it chase away the fear about her own mothering skills. Could her maternal instinct have been hampered or tainted by lack of bonding with her own mother?

One thing was certain, though. Simone would *never* strike a child—hers or anyone else's. So she wasn't the least bit afraid of that happening.

But would she have intimacy issues with her own son or daughter?

At this point, she hadn't heard a heartbeat or felt any movement. So it was hard to imagine a living, breathing child growing inside of her.

But there *was* a baby, a child who needed a loving mother.

Thirty minutes later, Dr. Wiley, the pediatrician on call, determined that the little girl's injury—nursemaid's elbow, he'd determined—was consistent with a normal parent/child incident and not a sign of abuse. And so there'd been nothing to report, which had filled Simone with a sense of relief. She was glad of the positive outcome for the family.

Isobel, who'd come to the E.R., was on her way back to her office, when she stopped to talk to Simone. "Did you have a chance to give those telephone numbers to your mother?"

"Yes. And she even admitted that she thought she needed some counseling, but when I told her that I knew about the date rape, she grew silent for a while. Then she started to cry, telling me she had to hang up. I have no idea what she'll do."

"Give her some time," Isobel said.

That's about all Simone could give her at this point. She'd taken the first step toward communicating with her mom on a different level, and now it was up to her mother to respond.

Was that what Mike was giving Simone? Some space and time to sort things out and decide what she needed to do?

Or was he making his own decision and trying to end their already rocky relationship?

That possibility sent a wave of nausea rolling through her tummy, and while the urge to call him grew stronger than ever, it was stilled by fear that it was too late.

Maybe she'd lost Mike already.

Mike arrived at the hospital at a little after four that afternoon, hoping Simone could take a break.

Over the past couple of days, he'd expected her to reach out to him. To miss him. To call.

But she hadn't.

He'd wanted to give her the time she needed and was willing to wait. But not if she didn't love him and didn't expect to ever have a future with him. If that was the case, he was spitting into the wind.

So the way he saw it, he'd been as patient as he could be. Now they needed to talk.

He entered the double doors that led to the waiting room, then stopped by the registration desk, while the woman in front of him signed in.

"I need to talk to Simone," he said when it was finally his turn. "Can you please tell her I'm here?"

The clerk, Carla Hawkins, nodded, then got up from her seat.

Mike stood to the side, arms crossed, and waited.

Several minutes later, Simone came to the window and motioned him to the security door, which she opened to let him inside.

"I need to talk to you," he said. "Can you take a break?"

Simone glanced at Jennifer, the LVN who was seated at the desk. "Can you cover for me a little while? I'll be in the garden. I have my pager, so let me know if you need me."

Jennifer nodded.

They walked side by side in silence to the door that led out to the hospital gardens, separated by more than the space between them.

Once outside, Mike crossed his arms and snared her gaze with his. "How do you feel about me?"

Her lips parted. "I…care about you. A lot."

"Do you love me?"

She seemed to ponder the question for a while, then slowly nodded. "I think so."

Damn. He'd told himself everything would be okay if she cared about him, if she thought she could grow to love him. But now he wasn't sure if what she might— or might not—be feeling would be enough.

"I want to create a family for our baby," he said. "And if marriage scares you, then I'm willing to try living together for a while. We can take things slow and easy, if you think that will help."

He studied her, watching for a sign that she was going to give in, that he'd somehow touched her heart. That he'd made her see that they were meant to be together. That they'd find a way to make things work.

Yet he feared that if she pulled back again…

Well, he wasn't sure what he'd do. There was always

plan B to fall back on, and as far as he was concerned, the ball was in her court.

Simone had her back to the open garden, yet she felt as though Mike had backed her into a corner. He was asking for a decision, a commitment.

And, apparently, he wanted it now.

"What exactly are you suggesting?" she asked. "That I give up my house and move into yours? That you let your new place fall out of escrow and move into mine?"

"I don't care either way. I'm willing to compromise. Are you?"

Was she? Quite frankly, she didn't know. She felt as though she were walking along a balance beam that stretched over a treacherous canyon.

The past was still etched too clearly in Simone's mind. Would she ever be able to forget her own childhood? Quiet all the doubts that tortured her? Put it all behind her and walk across that narrow beam that Mike swore led to a bright and happy future?

"I need an answer," he said.

She stiffened. Didn't he get it? Didn't he understand that she was in love with him? That she wanted to make that first step, but when he pressured her, she fell back into old habits and patterns?

"Don't push me," she said, unable to stop the words. "If it was just you and me, I'd consider it. But there's the baby to think about."

"What about the baby?"

"I'm afraid of failing it."

There it was. The horrible truth. The fear that loomed

over them both and prevented her from moving one way or the other on that precarious beam.

"Not *it*," he said, his tone a blend of anger and frustration. "You're pregnant with a little girl or boy just waiting to grow big enough to come out into the world."

"I realize that," she said, her voice growing softer, hesitant, and laden with what really concerned her. "But maybe he or she would be better off with another mother."

Mike bristled. "Are you still thinking about adoption?"

No, not as strongly as before. She now realized that while she feared she'd fail the baby somehow, she didn't want to give it up, either. Not to Millie, not to anyone.

"Damn it," Mike said, showing her a sign of righteous anger, of fierce determination he'd never fully revealed before. "You can get *that* thought out of your head right now."

What thought?

"My first plan was to marry you and create a home and family," he said. "But there are other options, and adoption isn't the only one. I'm not going to sign my son or daughter over to anyone. If you don't want it, I'll take the baby myself."

His words, his determination…his fierce loyalty, unbalanced her.

All along, she'd known Mike would be a fabulous father, but she hadn't thought he'd want to take the baby on his own. Or that he would be so determined, so adamant about it. And, if anything, she knew without a doubt that she would never give up her baby.

Not even to Mike.

"No, you—" Before she could finish telling him that he didn't understand, before she could explain that she wanted their child, too, a roaring buzz sounded in her ears, whizzing louder and louder.

And before she could utter a peep, the garden around them began to spin until her legs gave out and everything went dark.

Chapter Fourteen

Mike grabbed Simone just before she hit the ground, and he felt a rise of panic.

His training told him she'd had another fainting spell that was probably pregnancy related. But it wasn't easy being rational and detached from a patient when she was the woman he loved, a woman carrying the child they'd created.

Damn. Why had he pushed her?

Was he somehow to blame for this?

He dropped to his knees, taking her vitals, and watching her eyes flicker open. She moaned, and he felt both fear and relief.

"Mike?" she asked.

"Yes, honey. I'm here."

Her eyes searched his like a child awakening from a scary dream. "Please don't leave me."

"I won't," he said. And he meant it.

He could have called for help, but instead, he scooped her into his arms and carried her into the E.R., where he laid her on a gurney that had been parked in the hall. Then he wheeled her to the nurses' desk.

"Oh, God," Jennifer said. "What happened?"

"She fainted," Mike said. "Will you please call in an obstetrician?"

Jennifer's jaw dropped, and she paused for a beat before reaching for the phone.

"Call Dr. Kipper," Simone said softly.

Mike placed a hand on Simone's forehead, acknowledging that it was cool to the touch, then he caressed her hair, her cheek.

He'd pushed her too hard. But only because he loved her so much.

Moments later, an E.R. doctor hovered over Simone, checking vitals. The resident obstetrician, who explained he'd been sent by Dr. Kipper to make a preliminary exam, arrived and concurred with the diagnosis. The fainting spell had been a result of pregnancy, and Simone would be okay.

"Can we have an ultrasound?" Mike asked the obstetrician. "I want to make sure the baby's all right."

"Sure," the resident said. "I'll put in an order."

Mike stood beside the gurney and reached for Simone's hand. "I'm sorry for being so tough on you."

She gave his fingers a gentle squeeze. "You didn't cause me to faint, if that's what you mean."

"But I *did* upset you."

"Only because I'd begun to think you might be right about us. Then, before I could admit it to myself or to you, I felt you pulling away from me. And it was…more than a little unsettling. I can only imagine how you must have felt each time I did that to you."

Mike's heart took a tumble in his chest as he realized that they just might be able to work things out after all. "I wanted you and the baby to be a part of my life, and I tried to force your hand. I'm sorry."

"Apology accepted, but I'm afraid I owe you one, too. I love you, Mike. And that scares me. I've never had anyone love me back before."

Mike brushed a kiss across her lips. "It won't scare you for long. You're going to get used to it, to me. I promise. And as long as I know you love me, we can work it out."

"You've made a believer out of me."

She started to sit up, and he placed his hands on her shoulders and gently pushed her back down. "I'd feel better if you stayed still for a while. I don't want you passing out on me again."

Simone's gaze wrapped around his heart and held on tight. "I've never had anyone worry about me before."

Mike's grin brushed aside the concern on his face. "Then you'd better get used to it, honey. You've become a priority in my life. And I'm in this for the duration."

Simone studied the man who loved her, the man whose concern was so clearly written across his brow.

Isobel had said that trust was earned, and Mike had clearly earned hers. It was also a decision that was made. And today, at this very moment, she was going to consciously choose to trust Mike—now and forever.

You can't change the past, Isobel had said, *but you can change your perception of it.*

Simone realized her friend had been right. She'd thought that an emotionally distant mother and a bad childhood had been a millstone around her neck, an awkward set of baggage that would hold her down for the rest of her life.

But she'd come to realize that it had merely been one step in her life's journey, a journey that led her to Mike and the unconditional love she'd been craving for as long as she could remember.

"I can hardly believe it," she told him. "I'm going to create the family I never thought I could have—with you. It's going to be a new experience for me, so be patient."

"It's not so new. You've got a family of sorts in the hospital, people you respect and care about, people who respect and care about you, too."

He was right. She'd developed at least two close relationships with coworkers—Ella and Isobel.

But the most important relationship of all was the one she hadn't even expected, the one she had with Mike.

He loved her; he *really* loved her.

"What did I ever do to deserve you?" she asked.

He shot her a crooked grin. "You showed me the real Simone. And then I knew my bachelor days were over." He bent forward and brushed his lips across hers, gently but possessively. It was a kiss filled with promise.

"Excuse me," Jennifer said. "Simone, we're ready for that ultrasound."

Moments later, as Simone's belly was exposed and slathered with the cool gel, the resident obstetrician pointed to the black-and-white moving image on the screen.

"Everything looks good to me," he said.

Simone's breath caught, as her eyes focused on the form of a baby, its little heart pumping and beating strong, its arms and legs moving. A sense of awe filled her heart, her throat.

"Can you tell if it's a girl or boy yet?" Mike asked the doctor.

Simone turned her head to the doctor, listening intently. Suddenly, it mattered very much whether they would have a son or a daughter. She needed to start thinking about names and decorating a nursery.

"It's too soon to determine the baby's sex," the doctor said. "But what are you hoping for?"

"We don't care," Mike said, his eyes glistening with joy and wonder. "We just want the baby to be healthy."

He was right. Simone turned her head again, back to the screen. Back to their baby. And her own eyes filled with happy tears.

At that very moment, Simone knew that she would love their child no matter what sex it was, no matter who it looked like.

A bond had begun to form.

Or maybe it had begun to form the first time she'd looked into Mike's eyes and recognized the love that burned there.

"Well," said the doctor, "I think everything looks great and on schedule. Maybe you ought to just go home and take it easy for the rest of the day."

"Yes," Mike said. "Let's go home."

Simone had no idea if he was talking about his house or hers, but it no longer mattered.

Love was wherever Mike was.

* * *

On the way home, Mike mentioned that he needed to stop by his place and pick up Wags.

"Did you ever purchase more food for him?" Simone asked.

"Uh-oh. I meant to do that, but I haven't gotten around to it yet. Do you mind if I get some now? The pet shop is just ahead on Lexington."

"No, that's fine. It'll give me a chance to check on Millie. Fred said she had a flu bug that was giving her fits."

Moments later, Mike pulled in front of Tails a Waggin' and parked the Jeep. Once they'd both exited the vehicle, they walked hand in hand into the pet store.

Something felt very good and right about being with Mike, and Simone suspected that it wouldn't take any time at all for her to get used to being part of a couple.

When they entered the store, they'd agreed to separate, though. Mike went after the puppy food, and Simone wanted to say hello to Millie.

For the first time during one of her visits, she wasn't greeted by Popeye Baxter.

She spotted Millie, though.

Her friend was seated on a stool behind the cash register. She'd bent forward on the counter, where she was resting her head on her folded arms.

"Millie?" Simone asked. "Are you okay?"

The brunette looked up and managed a smile. "Oh, hi. I was just resting my eyes. I've been so tired lately that I find myself wanting to nap constantly."

"Are you still fighting that virus?"

"I'm afraid so." Millie blew out a weary sigh. "I just can't seem to kick it. Fortunately, it seems to come and go. But that's probably because of the excitement at our house these days."

"Fred mentioned you were going to have a few kids for a while. Are they still staying with you?"

"Yes, they are."

"How long are you going to have them?" Simone asked, wondering if Millie ought to be more concerned about her health.

"It's kind of a long story. Joe and Connie Prescott, a couple in our church, were foster parents for three small children. The girls are three and five. And the boy is nine. But when Joe had to transfer out of the country for business, they weren't going to be able to take the kids. Those poor little ones had been through a lot already, and the Prescotts hated to see them split up, which could have easily happened. It's so hard to find foster parents willing to take more than one child."

"Where are the kids now?" Simone asked.

"Greg, the boy, and Fred are at Little League practice. And Kimmy and Julie are with Gladys, Fred's mother. They're making cookies." Millie yawned. "Boy, I hope Fred gets back soon. I'd love to close up early and go home."

"Have the children found a permanent home yet?" Simone asked.

A broad smile stretched across Millie's face, dimpling her rosy cheeks. "As a matter of fact, they *have*. Fred and I have applied to be foster parents with the agreement that we eventually be allowed to adopt them."

"That's wonderful. How's it working out? I would imagine your lives are going to change dramatically."

Millie chuckled. "That's for sure. But Fred and I

don't mind a bit. And we couldn't be happier. The same goes for Popeye, who refuses to leave the children's side. The cats and the bird are still getting used to the hullabaloo, though. But I'm sure it won't take them very long."

"That's probably true."

"You know," Millie said, "I have to admit I was a bit worried about Fred's health. I hoped having the children wouldn't add too much stress to his life."

Simone nodded, sharing her friend's concern.

"But it's the weirdest thing. Since those kids came to live with us, Fred's coloring is much better, which leads me to believe that his heart condition is showing signs of improvement. I don't know if it's a divine miracle or just the result of sheer happiness. But we're not going to worry about it."

Simone wasn't sure what was going on, but she was glad to hear that Fred was feeling better.

"Now," Millie said, "if I could just kick this lingering virus that I've got, we'd all be happy. Thank goodness neither Fred nor the kids have caught it from me."

"What are your symptoms?" Simone asked.

"I seem to feel just fine when I wake up in the morning, but as the day wears on, I start feeling more and more nauseous. And I just seem to be tired all the time." She blew out a sigh. "But maybe juggling parenting duties with Fred and trying to work in the store has taken a bit of a toll on me. I'm sure I'll be feeling better soon."

"You're probably right." Still, Simone couldn't help wondering if the intermittent bouts of nausea and being tired might be pregnancy symptoms. She'd heard of cases where couples who'd been trying unsuccessfully to conceive for years finally gave up, only to find themselves pregnant when they least expected it.

But she didn't want to offer Millie false hope.

Either way, it seemed as though the Baxters had been granted the family they'd always dreamed of having.

Just as Simone had.

As Mike approached carrying a sack of puppy food, he tossed a smile Millie's way, greeting her. Then he waited as she rang up the charges.

After paying for their purchase, they were back in the Jeep and on their way to pick up Wags and take him home.

Home. Never had the word held so much love, so much hope.

Could Simone be any happier?

Ten minutes later, they arrived at Simone's house, and Mike carried Wags inside.

They still hadn't made any plans about where they would choose to live, but it seemed as though they had all the time in the world to decide.

Simone suspected they would live at her house while working together to fix up the old Dennison place. In the meantime, as the dogs played happily in the backyard, apparently glad to finally be together, she and Mike closed the back door and walked through the kitchen on their way to the bedroom.

He'd insisted that she lie down for a while and agreed to rest with her.

As was her habit, she glanced at the counter, where her answering machine sat, the red light indicating that she had a message.

So she stopped long enough to punch the play button and wait for the recording to sound.

"Simone? It's Mom. Please give me a call when you get in."

She glanced at Mike, who gave a little shrug. "If you decide to call now, maybe you should do it from the bedroom so you can at least put your feet up."

His concern for her well-being strummed something deep in her heart. "I feel fine, but if it makes you feel better, I'll lie down while I talk to her."

"It *does*," he said with a smile.

She returned her mother's call, and interestingly enough, they didn't have to play phone tag.

"Hey, Mom. It's me. What's up?"

"Oh hi, Simone. I just called to let you know that I spoke to one of the counselors you suggested."

"How did it go? Did you find it helpful?"

"As a matter of fact, I liked her. A *lot*. We had our first session last night, and I think it went…very well. I probably have a long way to go, but I wanted to thank you for encouraging me to contact her."

"I'm so glad you think she'll be helpful, Mom. And if you ever want or need to talk to me about it, you know you can, right?"

"Thanks, Simone. I know that I wasn't always there for you when you grew up, and I'm sorry. With Cynthia's friendship and Dr. Daniels's help, I'm hoping that things will…get better."

"I'd like that." Simone glanced at Mike, saw him watching her closely. Still, she wasn't sure if he knew how much this meant to her.

For as long as she could remember, she'd hoped

and prayed her mom would be normal, that they'd have what other mothers and daughters had. And she'd all but given up.

"I know I've never said it," her mother added, "but I do love you. And I want you to know that I blame myself for the bulk of the problems we've had. But I'm going to try and work on becoming a…better person, if not a better mother."

All she had any right to ask of her mother was that she at least try to get help. And, apparently, she was.

"I'm glad to hear it, Mom. And I have a few things that I probably ought to work on, too. I've pulled away a lot in the past, so it didn't help us find any common ground."

Silence stretched across the line, which Simone realized was par for the course for the two of them. But she hoped that, with time, the awkwardness would eventually lessen.

"While I have you on the line," Simone said, hoping her news would be helpful and not hinder her mother's progress, "there's something I want to tell you. I've fallen in love with a wonderful man. His name is Mike O'Rourke, and we plan to be married."

"That's…a nice surprise. I'm…happy for you. When is the wedding?"

"It's all in the planning stages now." Simone glanced at Mike and held on to the love glowing in his eyes. "I'll let you know when we decide on a date."

"Is he good to you?" her mother asked.

"Unbelievably so." Simone placed a hand on Mike's cheek and basked in all she'd found in his arms. "I'm the luckiest woman in the world."

"You deserve the best, Simone."

"Thanks, Mom." Simone chose to believe her mother was being sincere. "And, by the way, there's even more good news. We're also going to have a baby."

"A baby?"

"Yes, Mom. You're going to be a grandmother by the time next Christmas comes around."

"Imagine that. Time has a way of changing things."

Yes, it did.

They told each other goodbye and promised to chat again later, a promise that rang true.

Simone wasn't sure what the future would bring, but she was hopeful that, with counseling, her mom would work through the issues she should have taken care of right after the rape happened.

She knew she could never really change what had happened between them in the early years, but maybe her mother would be a better grandmother.

Mike kicked off his shoes, then stretched out upon the bed. He rolled to his side and patted the place beside him.

Words weren't needed. Simone was eager to curl up next to him. As much as she looked forward to making love again, the doctor had said to take it easy. And she didn't want to take any chances by overdoing it today.

So instead, she relished the feel of Mike's arms around her, the hint of his musky, male scent, the comfort that the gentle rise and fall of his chest provided.

"Do you know what?" Mike asked.

"What's that?"

"I recognize how hard you've worked to become the nurse that you are. So I don't expect you to be a stay-at-home mom unless you want to. I'm willing to either take care of the baby myself or juggle my schedule any way that will allow you to continue working."

She ran her fingertips along his cheek, felt the faint bristle of his beard. "You're a sweetheart, Mike O'Rourke. We'll just have to wait and see what the future brings." Then she cupped his jaw and pressed a kiss on his lips, allowing her hand to linger on his face. "Right now, I can't imagine wanting to give up my job completely, so I appreciate your willingness to work out a day-care solution."

"I'm sure my mom wouldn't mind helping out some, too. She loves babies."

That thought held a lot of appeal.

"You know," Simone said, "I like your mom. And your dad is great, too. I hope, when they get to know me better, that they'll feel the same way about me."

"They'll love you." He took her hand from his cheek and kissed her palm. "And so will the rest of my family. As big and boisterous as the O'Rourkes can sometimes be, they've always welcomed each new in-law and baby with open arms. So you'll be one of them, too."

A family of her own. Imagine that.

"I love you," Simone said, enjoying the sound of her words and realizing they came easier each time she said them.

"I love you, too."

They lay like that for a while, caught up in the intimacy they shared. An intimacy Simone no longer found the least bit scary. Not with Mike.

"Thanks for seeing something inside my cool exterior," she said. "And for being persistent about making me see it, too."

"I didn't have to look that deep. I've got an eye for inner warmth and beauty."

Simone smiled, her heart swelling to the bursting point.

Mike had set his sights on her, just as he had that old Victorian on Maple Drive that he'd purchased. He'd sensed what a little tender loving care could do and was determined to renovate the run-down house into a happy home.

There was no doubt that he would succeed.

After all, that's exactly what he'd done with Simone's heart.

* * * * *

THE WILDER FAMILY *continues next month!*
*Spring fever hits Walnut River! When social
worker Isobel Suarez reluctantly teams up with
investigator Neil Kane to root out a mole in the
hospital, late nights and close quarters lead
to shared kisses…but will true love bloom?*

Find out in Her Mr Right?
*by Karen Rose Smith,
on sale May 2009 wherever
Mills & Boon® books are sold.*

Mills & Boon® Special Edition
brings you a sneak preview of Christine Rimmer's
In Bed with the Boss,
which is available in May 2009.

Little did hotel-chain CFO Tom Holloway realise
that his new executive assistant spelled trouble.
But even though single mum Shelly Winston was
planted by Holloway's worst enemy to take him
down, Shelly was no fool – she had a mind of her
own and an eye for her handsome boss!

Don't miss this exciting new story coming next
month from Mills & Boon® Special Edition!

In Bed with the Boss

by

Christine Rimmer

Two years ago...

It was *the* moment.

And Tom Holloway knew it.

Across the black granite boardroom table, Helen Taka-Hanson waited, her beautiful face composed, showing him nothing. Behind her, beyond the floor-to-ceiling windows, the afternoon sun reflected off the tall buildings of North Michigan Avenue. Tom kept his gaze level, on Helen. But he knew what was out there: The Second City. The Magnificent Mile.

Chicago. Tom wanted it. *Needed* it, really. A fresh start in a new town. He would be chief financial officer of TAKA-Hanson's new hospitality division.

Which meant hotels. Contemporary luxury hotels on a grand scale. It was the biggest venture he'd tackled so far and it sounded good. Better than good.

And the job was his. Helen had already made the offer.

What he said next could blow it for him—more than likely *would* blow it for him. Which was why he'd left the crucial information off his résumé. His disgrace had happened so long ago, it was easily glossed over now.

But Tom had learned the hard way that concealment didn't work in the long term. The high-stakes world of finance was too damn small. In the end, his past always found him.

Better to show his stuff first, let them know he had the chops, get all the way to the job offer. And then take a deep breath and lay the bad news right out there.

The offer just might stand in spite of his past. If it didn't, if he lost the job, well, chances were he would have lost it anyway in the end, when the ugly facts surfaced.

Oh, yeah. A delicate moment, this. The moment of truth.

Helen said, "Well, Tom. You've heard our offer. Is there anything else we need to go over?"

Tom sat back in the chair, ordered his body to relax and told himself—for the hundredth time—that it had to be done.

"As a matter of fact, Helen. There is something else…"

She arched a brow at him and waited for him to go on.

He said, "I was fired once. It was a long time ago, my first job out of Princeton."

"Fired." Helen spoke the word flatly. "That's not on your résumé, is it?"

"No. And it gets worse."

"I'm listening."

"I was young and way too hungry, working on Wall Street, determined to make it big and do it fast. None of which is any justification for my actions. I was discharged for insider trading. And then I was arrested for it. And convicted. I did six months."

A silence. A pretty long one. Tom could feel yet another great job slipping away from him.

At last, Helen asked the big question. "Were you guilty?"

"Yes. I was."

He might have softened the harsh fact a little. He could have explained what a naive idiot he'd been then. He could have told her all about his mentor at the time, who'd convinced him to pass certain "tips" to big clients. He could have said that the guy got away clean by setting Tom up to take the fall for him. That the same former mentor had been a curse on his life since then. Because of that one man, Tom had lost out on a number of opportunities—and not just in terms of his career. It would have been the truth.

However, his former boss wasn't the one up for CFO, TAKA-Hanson, hospitality division. Tom was. His prospective employer needed to know that he'd once broken the law—and then gone to jail for it. The why and the wherefore?

Not the question.

Tom sat unflinching, waiting for the ax to fall.

Instead, Helen smiled.

It was a slow smile, and absolutely genuine—a warm smile, the kind of smile that would make any red-blooded man sit up and take notice. From what Tom had heard, this genius of the business world, now in her late forties, had saved Hanson Media from collapse several years back, after her first husband, George Hanson, died suddenly. The story went that before she was forced to step in and save the family business, she'd been a trophy wife.

Smart and savvy and strictly professional as she'd been since he met her, Tom had been having trouble seeing her as mere arm candy for a tycoon. But now he'd been granted that amazing smile, he wasn't having trouble anymore.

That face, that smile…

George Hanson had been one lucky man. And so was her current husband, TAKA-Hanson's chairman of the board, Morito Taka.

"I prize honesty," Helen said. "I prize it highly. So I think it's time I repaid your truth with one of my own. I've done my homework on you, Tom. I've known all along about how you lost that trading job, and the price you paid for what you did. I've been interested to see if you'd tell me about it. And now that you have, I'm more certain than ever on this. Other than that one admittedly serious black mark against you—for which you've paid your dues—your record is spotless. I know you'll make a fine addition to my team. I've got no reservations. You're the man for this job."

Tom's heart slammed against his breastbone. Had he

heard right? Had it worked out, after all? The CEO knew the truth.

And she'd hired him anyway.

He held out his hand. Helen took it. They shook.

When he spoke, his voice was firm and level. "I intend to make sure you never regret this decision."

"I believe you," said Helen. "That's another reason you're our new CFO."

On sale 17th April 2009

The Millionaire's Makeover
by Lilian Darcy

Of all of Rowena Madison's demanding clients, businessman Ben Radford took the cake. But as the work on his exotic garden bought them closer together, love began to blossom between them!

The Doctor Next Door
by Victoria Pade

When Faith comes back from the big city, Boone has the chance to make her see that their home town is the ideal place for settling down – together.

Dad in Disguise
by Kate Little

Thanks to a medical mistake, Jack Sawyer now had a son. When Jack went undercover to check on his baby, he lost his heart – to Rachel, the boy's mother! But when the dad took off his disguise, all hell broke loose…